THE RESETTLEMENT OF ISAAC

ISBN 978-0-912887-67-8
LCCN 2020941346

Designed by Lauren Grosskopf, Publisher / Designer
Lauren@pleasureboatstudio.com

*Pleasure Boat Studio books are available
through your favorite bookstore & through the following:*

PLEASURE BOAT STUDIO: A LITERARY PRESS
PLEASUREBOATSTUDIO.COM | SEATTLE, WASHINGTON &
BAKER & TAYLOR, INGRAM, AMAZON.COM & BN.COM

THE RESETTLEMENT OF ISAAC

A TRUE LOVE STORY

by ROBERT KARMON

PLEASURE BOAT STUDIO: A LITERARY PRESS

CAST OF CHARACTERS

ISAAC: A Polish Jew in his seventies who miraculously survived a Nazi massacre as a young man, joined a Russian Partisan Brigade, and fell in love.

ANYA/ANNA: Anya, a Christian, is a Russian Partisan nurse in World War Two / Anna is an unemployed Elementary School Teacher in 1998 who lives in her late mother's rent-controlled apartment on Manhattan's Upper West Side. She is a German-American Christian. Both characters are played by the same actor. 29-years old.

YOUNG ISAAC: 17-years old. Isaac's younger self who calls himself Sergei to hide his Jewish identity. He joins Anya's Russian Partisan Brigade pretending to be a Russian Christian and falls in love with her.

JOSEF: Anna's 35-year old German-American wealthy brother. He can also double as the German Commandant Bichel.

MERCEDES: A 40-50 year-old Hispanic nursing supervisor at a New York Nursing Home. She can also double as Lyuba, Sol's wife.

WASIC: A 25-30 year old Russian fighting the Nazis in the same Brigade as Isaac and Anya. He does not appear until the Second Act. He can also double as Sol, Young Isaac's beloved older brother, as well as Polish Policeman and First Young Man.

KCHOLP: A 26-year old Polish fireman and Young Issac's Christian neighbor. He can also play Hospital Orderly and Second Young Man.

ALYOSHA: A rugged 40-50 year old Russian Partisan demolition expert. He can also play Lazar, Young Isaac's resolute and hopeful Father, as well as The Male Passerby.

A NOTE

The Character of Isaac and his love for Anya is inspired by a real and remarkable Isaac, a survivor of the Rovno Massacre, who became a demolition expert for the Russian Partisan Brigade and an American hero, after saving the lives of American soldiers.

The play can be performed in English or as a multilingual production. In a multilingual performance, actors will speak the language indicated in the script. Simultaneous translations into English of those scenes will occur with the help of wireless head-sets, similar to those used by theaters for the hard of hearing.

STAGING

A unit set with a table, two chairs, a bench, some platforms, a door, a bed, and a small wooden stool along with creative lighting, some music and projections. Even though the scenes shift from the 1940's to 1998, the different settings do not require anything more than the slightest variation in costuming.

from the
PLAYBILL

MONDAY, AUGUST 21ST 2018 AT 7 P.M.
25 Pond Lane – Southampton, N.Y.

**SOUTHAMPTON CULTURAL CENTER
THIRD ANNUAL JEWISH FILM FESTIVAL**
In Association With
THE PLAYWRIGHTS' THEATER OF EAST HAMPTON
Presents a Staged Reading of
THE RESETTLEMENT OF ISAAC
A New Play by
ROBERT KARMON

CAST IN ORDER OF APPEARANCE

ISAAC	**Jeremy Lawrence***
MALE PASSERBY / LAZAR	**Mitchell W. Robin**
ANYA / ANNA	**Annemarie Hagenaars**
MERCEDES	**Mary Francina Golden***
YOUNG ISAAC	**Michael Quattrone***
JOSEF / EINSATZGRUPPEN KOMMANDANT BICHEL /	
WASEK / YOUNG MAN I	**Robert Meksin***
SOL / YOUNG MAN II	**Michael Cruise**
LYUBA	**Carolyn A. Chichester**
KCHLOP / ALYOSHA	**John Fitzgibbon***
READER: STAGE DIRECTIONS	**Marsha Lee Sheiness**

Directed by ROBERT KALFIN **

* Member – Actors Equity Association
** Member – Society of Stage Directors & Choreographers

MICHAEL CRUISE grew up in New York City and began acting after college. He was the lead singer and dancer in "Blind Dog Ballet," an Electronic/Metal group with heavily featured and choreographed dancing. He produced, composed and recorded all of the music and produced and directed the stage show. He was involved in "The Thomas Crown Affair," and "Oz." He has also starred in several Independent Film Projects including "Dan the Martial Arts Man," as Dan, and "Prelude to Genesis," as Adam/Drexar, a production he also wrote and directed. He can play the guitar, bass, drums, and of course, sing.

JOHN FITZGIBBON (Kchlop/Alyosha) He first worked with Bob Kalfin in Genet's SCREENS in 1971; then A PASSIONATE WOMAN (opposite Loretta Swit at the Cocoanut Grove); and then SHANGHAI GESTURE (55th St Theatre). He has been on Broadway and Off-Broadway and in theatres stretching from Hawaii to Greece: 13 new plays at NJ Rep (SuzAnne Barabas, artistic director); 18 plays directed by Stuart Vaughan (New Globe Theatre); 5 at the Caldwell Theatre, Florida; 5 at the Shakespeare Theatre of New Jersey; 10 and the Barter Theatre, Virginia; Favorite role: "Jim Tyrone" in Moon for the Misbegotten (Best of Boston Award). He is also a pianist/composer and his CD: "REFLECTIONS" can be sampled at CDBaby.com.

MARY FRANCINA GOLDEN (AEA, SAG/AFTRA) Oxford Shakespeare Company (New York, London, Edinburgh, Venice); New Globe Theatre (Stuart Vaughan); Trinity Rep (Adrian Hall); Pennsylvania Stage; Asolo Theatre; HB Playwrights Foundation, among others. *As You Like It; Hedda Gabler; 'Night Mother; Talley's Folly; Rimers of Eldridge* (Amy Wright); *Romeo and Juliet; Alls Well That Ends Well; MacBeth; Merchant of Venice; Ghosts* (Kim Hunter); *Importance of Being Earnest; Glass Menagerie.* Ms. Golden produced and acted in *The Sun Shines East,* Corinne Chateau's critically acclaimed play about foreign adoption. She has appeared in the award-winning Indie short "The Tailor", several web series, and several Soaps. Training: MFA (Catholic U.); Patsy Rodenburg, John Barton, Cicely Berry; Austin Pendleton, George Morfogen.

ANNEMARIE HAGENAARS is thrilled to be part of the ISAAC cast. It's her first time in the Hamptons. Annemarie moved to NYC in March 2016 from the Netherlands. She is a member of the WorkShop Theater Company. She recently worked on Charles Leipart's play *Chez Rikers* alongside Penny Fuller and Tony Roberts. In April 2017 she performed in her first Off Broadway show *CasablancaBox* (two Drama

Desk Awards nominations). She also performed in various productions with Radio Theatre NYC and works as a VO artist. She played Nell McNally in *The Country House* and booked TV roles on *Homicide for the Holidays* and *Mysteries at The Museum*. www.annemariehagenaars.nl

ROBERT KALFIN [DIRECTOR] has directed over 500 plays, including works on Broadway - [HAPPY END with Christopher Lloyd and Meryl Streep; YENTL with Tovah Feldshuh; STRIDER - THE STORY OF A HORSE], as well as Off-Broadway, regional theaters, in countries abroad as far as Siberia, and on the PBS Great Performances Series, "Theater In America." [THE PRINCE OF HOMBURG starring Frank Langella]. Founder / Artistic Director of the Tony Award winning Chelsea Theater Center for the Hal Prince production of CANDIDE, in 2015 he was honored as "An Off-Broadway Legend." His book for young directors, MAKING IT SAFE TO BE UNSAFE, is currently being edited for publication.

ROBERT KARMON is an award-winning American playwright, screenwriter and poet. Several of his plays have been produced off-Broadway and in regional theaters, including Playwrights Horizon, Urban Stages and Minneapolis' Tyrone Guthrie Theatre. He was a member of Edward Albee's Playwrights Unit. Karmon's screenwriting credits include scripts for CBS, Columbia Pictures and Eddie Murphy Productions. This play, "The Resettlement of Isaac," is based in part on his historical fiction novel, "Isaac."

JEREMY LAWRENCE His critically acclaimed *Lavender Songs: A Queer Weimar Berlin Cabaret* will be revived in October at Pangea www.pangeanyc.com. In late September, he will be in the TOSOS Theatre Company's much heralded production of *Street Theatre*. www.tososnyc.org. Recent TV: *The Blacklist* and *Shades of Blue*. New York theatre includes: Manhattan Theatre Club and 4 shows for the Mint Theatre. Regional: *Fiddler* (Goodspeed, the MUNY), *Noises Off* (Actors Theatre of Louisville), *Into The Woods* (Baltimore Center Stage and Westport Country Playhouse), and also *Tartuffe* at Westport. He is the perennial "Scrooge" for the the 2300 seat Hanover Theater, Worcester, MA. Film credits: *Critters*, work with Stephen Daldry, Ron Howard and Brian DePalma. His one man Tennessee Williams shows have received international acclaim. www.jeremylawrence.net

MITCHELL W. ROBIN This is the second time that Mitch (aka Dr. Mitch) has performed in an original play at Center Stage. The first was in "Mom its My Wedding" (Father of the Bride) by Ilene Beckerman and Michael Disher. He has also been seen in LTV's production of *L'il Abner* (General Bullmoose) as well as in RFCT's production of *42nd St* (Abner Dillon) When he is between performances Dr. Mitch can be found at his day job in either Manhattan or Hampton Bays where he "performs" as a licensed NYS Psychologist.

MARSHA LEE SHEINESS' plays have been produced Off-Broadway, Off-Off Broadway, Television, Regional, Community, University, and High Schools, also in Japan, Canada, England, and New Zealand. Awards: National Endowment for the Arts for Playwriting: Actress, Director, Playwriting teacher. Member: Dramatist Guild, WGE, PEN, AEA, SAG. Publishers: Dramatic Publishing, Samuel French, Inc., Art-Age, and Blue Moon Plays. Represented by Leo Bookman, (212) 472-8976. See Marshasheiness.com

THE PLAYWRIGHTS THEATER OF EAST HAMPTON

Mitzi and Perry Pazer, founders of the Playwrights Theater of East Hampton, have presented 64 new plays over 21 years, helping writers to develop their work in rehearsed public readings. Reading over 100 plays each year, Mitzi selects 4 for presentation each summer with transportation, housing, meals and a small stipend provided for all participants. The only stipulation is that the playwright be available for rehearsals and post-performance audience discussions. They are delighted to be Co-Presenters of THE RESETTLEMENT OF ISAAC with the Southampton Cultural Center's Third Annual Jewish Film Festival.

Dedication

I REMAIN DEEPLY GRATEFUL FOR THE ABIDING AFFECTION AND
PATIENCE OF MY DEAR WIFE, KAY, THE UPLIFTING PRESENCE OF MY
DAUGHTERS, ELYSA AND JENNIFER, THEIR CARING HUSBANDS,
HARRY AND JOHN, AND THE INIMITABLE CHARM AND SMILES OF MY
GRANDCHILDREN, JESSE, ZOE AND ELLE.

THANKS IS DUE TO THE GENEROUS AND SUPPORTIVE PRESENCE
OF MY EDITOR AND PUBLISHER, LAUREN GROSSKOPF.

MUCH ARTISTIC GRATITUDE AS WELL TO MY MENTOR AND GIFTED
DIRECTOR, ROBERT KALFIN, WHO GUIDED ME THROUGH TO THE
THEATRICAL HEART AND SOUL OF THE PLAY.

FINALLY, I AM FOREVER INDEBTED TO THE ENDURING SPIRIT,
INSPIRATION AND MEMORY OF ISAAC GOCHMAN.

ACT ONE

SCENE ONE

(Cold Winter Night. 1998. New York. Riverside Park, overlooking
the Hudson River, Upper West Side.)

(Isaac, 73, sits on his park bench, holding a mahogany cane topped
with an ornate brass handle. He wears a ragged Russian mouton
cap with ear flaps. He is covered from shoulder to ankle by a frayed
and faded long coat hiding the fact that he is wearing just boxer
shorts and an undershirt beneath the coat. On his lap is a frayed
cloth satchel.)

(The bench overlooks the Hudson River, swollen by recent rains.
It is near a well-traveled bridge. Isaac thinks he hears the sound of
rushing water, interrupted from time to time by the very real sound
of the clattering wheels of cars going across the bridge which
sound like marching boots to Isaac.)

(His face is marred by a deep scar across his forehead, but his eyes
reveal an inextinguishable vitality in spite of his aging, world-weary
body. He seems to be waiting for someone to appear. Lights dim.
Sound of rushing water triggers Isaac's memory.)

(He puts cane aside and reaches into his satchel and pulls out an
old East European map. It is crumpled and difficult to handle. He
spreads it out on his lap, looking intensely for some location, but
his eyes fail him. He struggles with the map. It slips off his lap, and
he hurriedly goes to his knees to recover it from the ground. He is
kneeling when he imagines Anya.)

(Anya, 29, a beautiful Russian woman, appears in Isaac's memory
as if emerging up from the river. She wears a leather vest, a dark
cap, fatigues and carries a rifle strapped to her shoulder. Isaac sees
her. He is startled. Looks at her.)

(They speak in Russian throughout their scene.)

ISAAC

Anya?

(He grabs the map, then leaning on his cane, he struggles to get up, but has difficulty standing. Kneels down again painfully on one knee, holding on to cane to keep his balance. He imagines the sound of rushing water.)

ANYA

(Loudly)

Sergei!

(Isaac looks around as if someone heard her.)

What are you doing kneeling? That's not like you. Did you forget me?

ISAAC

No, Anya! Never!

(He struggles once more with the help of his cane and raises himself up. Then collapses, sitting back on the bench.)

ANYA

Now, now, Sergei, enough of that. Hurry, little cricket. Very little time. Very little. Don't forget to get far enough away before the train explodes. But then you know all that. Remember it's a short fuse Alyosha put in your satchel. It's always a short fuse.

ISAAC

A short fuse?

ANYA

Don't forget. Meet me as usual by the eddies where the rivers cross.

(Isaac looks endearingly at Anya.)

(Lights begin to fade on her.)

Hurry. The Nazis are retreating from Mother Russia. The war will be over soon.

(Isaac keeps looking at her.)

Sergei? Are you listening? Soon we'll be together. Yes? No more hiding. Yes?

ISAAC

No more. Yes.

ANYA
> Come back, safe and sound. Promise.

ISAAC
> Yes. Safe and sound. Promise.

ANYA
> Safe and sound. For me. For us. No time left. Hurry.

(Lights fade on her.)
> I'll be waiting.

(She is gone.)

ISAAC
> Anya! Anya, don't go. Help me. "Skolko Vremeni?"

(Then in Yiddish)
> How much time…?

(Sound of cars clattering over bridge and honking of horns drown out the sound of rushing water.)
(Isaac grabs the map and, painfully, with the help of his cane, he stands, looking for Anya.)
(Male passerby is seen, back to Isaac. He wears a ski cap and puffy ski jacket. Isaac approaches him, thinking he knows him, but confused by his outfit. He taps him on the shoulder and speaks to him in Russian.)

ISAAC
> Alyosha? Eto ty? Is it really you?

(Male passerby turns. He is a stranger to Isaac.)

MALE PASSERBY (IN ENGLISH)
> What the hell kind of language are you talking?

ISAAC
> I thought…No!…

(He speaks in English.)
> I'm sorry, sir. I am looking for this.

(He holds out the map.)
> What is the name of this village?

MALE PASSERBY
> Village? You mean like Greenwich Village? It's way

downtown, old man.

ISAAC

No. This has to be Rovno here. Yes? Rovno. Poland. I'm looking for Brovary, near Kyev Ostrov. Many kilometers west of here. See? Yes? Look at the map. My eyes are not so good. Look, please. Now that the war is over, I must get back to my Anya.

(Man takes the East European map. Holds it up and down and realizes it has nothing to do with where they are.)

MALE PASSERBY

What war did you say?

ISAAC

The war! Against Hitler, against the Nazis. It's over. It's been over for a year. Everyone knows.

MALE PASSERBY

That war? That's ancient history. You must be kidding, man.

ISAAC

Can you tell me? I need to find the way to Brovary near Kyev. I am near? Yes?

MALE PASSERBY

Are you nuts? Near what? This map's a joke! What freakin' planet are you from?

(He laughs in Isaac's face. Gives the map back.)

Old man, you're way off. Way off. It's 1998, Pop, Manhattan. Get it? That's the Hudson. There's the George Washington Bridge. You're somewhere else. Seriously. Get a grip.

(He shakes his head and is gone.)

ISAAC

(Stands, a bit unsteady, leaning on his cane.)

No. No.

(He falls back onto the bench. Spreads map on his lap. Puts finger on what he thinks is Anya's town.)

Here! Here! Brovary! Very near.

(A moment passes as he catches his breath.)
(Anna, 29, appears on stage. She has thrown a winter coat over a bathrobe.
She should be the same actor who plays Anya.)
(She carries a stadium blanket with her.)
(They speak in English.)

ANNA
**Issac, I saw you from my window. It's deathly cold out
here. You're going to freeze if you don't come inside.**
(Her quiet voice is muffled by the sound of cars honking; Isaac doesn't see
or hear her.)
Here. This will help.
(She drapes a blanket over his shoulder. He stands up as if to defend
himself. Looks at her.)

ISAAC
Anya?

ANNA
No. I'm Anna.

ISAAC
Anna?

ANNA
I didn't mean to frighten you.

ISAAC
It's just…nothing.
(Begins to realize where he is.)
Forgive me.

ANNA
I thought you might be cold so I brought…

ISAAC
You shouldn't have.

ANNA
Why don't you come inside with me?

ISAAC

**I'll be fine. I do know you, don't I? But you look like
someone else.**
(Looks around.)
I think I've lost my way.

ANNA

**It's all right. You live right over there. I'm across the hall
from you. You gave me your key just in case. Remember?**

ISAAC

I did?

ANNA

Come. I'll make you some tea.

ISAAC

You're not Anya?

ANNA

No. I…I wish I was. No. Just Anna.

ISAAC

She called me Sergei. Like I remember, just before…

ANNA

You told me many times.

ISAAC

Sergei. Yes. And you are Anya.

ANNA

Come. Inside.

ISAAC
(Looking inside his satchel.)
**Wait. I've saved such a gift for you.
From the last German train I blew up.**
(Looks for it but his satchel is only filled with his yellow
handwritten pages.)
Where is it? I saved it just for you…A German service

medal, pure silver. I don't understand. Where…?
(Anna shakes her head.)

ANNA

You'll find it later. I'm sure. Later

ISAAC

But when? When, Anya?

ANNA

Please try and understand, I'm Anna. Not Anya. Come.
Please.

ISAAC
(To Anna.)
Anna? How much time, Anna?
(In Russian.)
Skolko vremeni?
(Blanket starts to slip off Isaac, but Anna keeps it from falling off him. He
starts crying, shivering, frightened. Anna holds him, trying to comfort him.
He clutches the map tightly. (Mumbles in Yiddish as he clings to her with
the map still in his hand.)
Vos? Vos?
(Lights fade)

SCENE TWO

(Next afternoon. Nursing home. Outside Isaac's room.)
(Lights up on Anna in her winter coat and Mercedes, a
Hispanic Nursing Home Supervisor and Head Nurse.)
(They speak in English.)

MERCEDES

Your brother called ahead to assure us he would cover all
expenses. Did you hear me?

ANNA

Yes. I know. I told him it was what I wanted.

MERCEDES

We will take good care of him.

ANNA

This sleep of his? What do you make of all his
twisting and turning? That's not rest at all.

MERCEDES

I know this may sound a bit harsh, but very few in here
sleep soundly through the night. More often than not,
we have to give them something to quiet their nerves.

ANNA

Have you given him anything?

MERCEDES

First, I have to know, what is your relationship to Mr.
Hochman, Mrs…?

ANNA

Miss Brown. I'm a caring neighbor of many years.
A good friend.

MERCEDES

You must be his only friend. No one else has shown up

or called except you and…your brother.

ANNA

Isaac has no family. When he moved in right across the hall from me, his wife was not well. She died soon after and he never mentioned children.

MERCEDES

It's sad but so many in here have outlived everyone they knew or loved. Isaac is lucky to have you and your brother.

ANNA

He doesn't have my brother. I have my brother and I have to twist his arm to have him help Isaac.

MERCEDES

I promise we'll do all we can to make him comfortable but you have to understand, many patients like him might end up upstairs in lockdown.

ANNA

Lockdown?

MERCEDES

Trust me, it's the last resort. For the patient's safety and security. Only when they have become a danger to themselves.

ANNA

No! Never! Not Isaac!

MERCEDES
(Comforts her.)

It's the last resort, I promise. Don't give it another thought.

ANNA

Thank you.

MERCEDES

So what made you bring him to us?

ANNA

> Last night, I saw the door to his apartment wide open and I knew he had wandered outside like so many times before. This time, though, when I got to him, he was crying and so lost, I don't think he even remembered where he lived. I knew then he needed more help than I could give him.

MERCEDES

> It tears you apart when you see them crying like that, doesn't it? I look in their faces and see my blessed mother and father, the strong ones who keep families together, suddenly breaking down, helpless. And I want to cry with them.

(Crosses herself.)

> I don't let myself, of course. But still…

ANNA

> So I know he needs professional care. Just not lockdown. Not that! Please!

MERCEDES

> It's for their own security. Believe me. Last month I lost one of my patients just like that. He took off in the middle of the night. Security must have been sleeping at the door…and the next day they found him.

ANNA

> Thank god.

MERCEDES

> No. No thanks at all. He drowned in the river.
> Must have walked straight off a pier…

(Crosses herself.)

ANNA

> Poor man. It's just not right.

(Emphatic.)

> It's different with Isaac. I'll always be here for him.
> Just keep him safe, comfortable. It's personal.

MERCEDES

Personal?

ANNA

Many times in the past I'd bring him some hot soup and then one day he lifted out of his satchel a bundle of yellow papers and gave them to me to read.

MERCEDES

I don't follow.

ANNA

He had written down all he remembered from the war on those yellow pages. I don't know if he wrote it all down because he was afraid he would forget or that he was finally ready to remember. He told me he had never shown anyone those pages before. Not even to his late wife, Sarah.

MERCEDES

I see.

ANNA

He shared so much with me. Look at this photo he gave me from the war.

(Gives Nurse one photo.)

MERCEDES

Vietnam?

(Music begins. Slow, cross-fading projections of Isaac's yellowing hand-written pages and an old faded photo of young Isaac as a Partisan fighter.)

ANNA

No. World War Two, fighting with Russian Partisans against the Nazis.

(Points at figures in photo.)

See! He's that young boy with the dark cap. And the one next to him, with her rifle over her shoulder, wearing that jacket with the dark fur, he calls her Anya. Like he sometimes calls me.

MERCEDES

It's turning yellow.

ANNA

He's written it all down. You can't imagine what he has been through.

MERCEDES

Just a word of caution. This place is full of stories that make no sense. Woman down the hall told me she was once a Duchess in England. Lived in a Castle. Found out she watched nothing all day but those English shows on the public channels. I loved those shows myself. Whenever I could sneak a peek. But she really thought it was all about her. Sadly there are no castles in the real world for her, for any of us. We'll have to move her upstairs into Lockdown. For her own good. Believe me.

ANNA

That's not where Isaac belongs!
(Music, projections and photo fade out.)

MERCEDES
(Preparing to leave.)

Trust us to take good care of him, Mrs. Brown.

ANNA

It's Miss Brown. Call me Anna.

MERCEDES

Anna.

ANNA

And yours? Oh, I see. Mercedes. Like the car.
(Looks on name tag.)

MERCEDES

No. In Spanish, it means "many mercies."

ANNA

That's beautiful.

MERCEDES
I'd rather have the car than the name.
(They laugh.)

ANNA
That's what he needs.

MERCEDES
A car?

ANNA
No. Mercy. Compassion. Make sure everyone treats him well.

MERCEDES
I will make sure. Promise.
(Hands photo back to Anna.)

ANNA
Here's my phone number and Isaac's.

MERCEDES
Why Isaac's?

ANNA
I might be in his apartment to gather some things for him.
He gave me his key. Call me about any changes. But...
now...it's best I let him sleep, right?
(Lights up on nursing bed with restless figure under the blanket.)

MERCEDES
I wouldn't wake him.

ANNA
Take good care of him. Please, Mercedes.
He needs, he deserves...many mercies.
(Nurse smiles and nods, taking her hand to reassure her.)
(Anna exits, Mercedes stands watching.)

MERCEDES
(To herself, sighing.)
It's all the same when they end up here.
(Crosses herself.)
(Lights fade on Mercedes.)

SCENE THREE

(Lights up on Isaac's apartment. Anna is sitting on the kitchen table holding Isaac's satchel. Isaac's mahogany cane leans against the table. Anna is clearly upset by her decision to take Isaac to a nursing home. She gets up, holding the satchel, picks up the cane as if she is going to go back and bring Isaac home again. Then, thinking better of it, she sits down. She pulls out some of Isaac's handwritten accounts of his life as a partisan. She starts to read.)
(Lights up on Old Isaac sitting on a small wooden stool on the side of the stage, in his long coat and Russian Mouton hat, with his cane leaning against the stool.)
(We hear the sound of rushing water. Music swells. Projection of Isaac's yellowing handwritten pages.)
(Lights fade on Anna. Isaac talks to the audience, speaking the words that Anna is reading.)

ISAAC

> Anya promised to come to me once more by the eddies where the rivers cross. We had been meeting here for many months. The first time we came together months ago, it was all so new to me, this lovemaking, this feeling of intimacy with a woman. Even after being with her many times, I still felt like a fumbling innocent, clumsy and inept.

(Cross fade out of music and projections.)
(The sound of rushing water continues.)
(Lights up on Young Isaac, 17. He is kneeling by the river, washing his face, his Russian hat by his side.)

> While waiting for Anya, I would splash cold water on my face. It was all anyone dare do in this Partisan Out-post. No one ever undressed given the bitter cold and the constant danger of attacks. And there was always the chance someone would steal your clothes. From time to time I would sprinkle myself with DDT powder to keep clean. Anya would often sniff around me and think I was wearing some strange new cologne.

(Young Isaac puts on his hat then takes it off and starts playing with the buttons of his jacket, while he waits nervously for Anya.)

That first time we became intimate, I wondered how we could ever fit together through all our clothes. I couldn't imagine lovemaking with all those buttons and snaps and zippers in the way. Maybe, I thought, maybe I should be thankful she could not see me from the waist down. But, maybe, this was the time I would tell her who I really was.

(Young Isaac fidgets with his buttons again. Takes off his hat and tries to smooth down his hair.)

(Lights up on Anya, 29, entering the scene. She is dressed in her Partisan outfit from Scene One. She watches Isaac and smiles. He sees her and nervously smiles back.)

Then I saw her coming towards me and all I wanted was to be close to her again. The truth would have to wait once more.

(Anya walks to him, strokes his face and then kisses him passionately. As Young Isaac embraces her, he and Old Isaac look at each other across the stage in seeming recognition, memory bridging the gulf of time.)

(Lights fade on lovers.)

(Lights dim on old Isaac remembering, still watching.)

(Sound of rushing water increases.)

SCENE FOUR

(Music for a moment. The lights fade up on Young Isaac
with his shirt half open.)
(Anya, 29, enters after him. She is zipping up her fur-lined jacket.
Young Isaac, 18 starts buttoning his shirt but Anya stops him. She
lifts his shirt to examine his back.)
(Old Isaac watches the scene.)
(They speak in Russian.)

ANYA

Sergei, your poor wounds. Are they healing?
I did the best I could with what we had.

(She touches his scarred back. Some wounds are still red.)

YOUNG ISAAC

No matter how badly I'm hurt, I always come to you
first. You are my first for everything.

(He takes her hand, kisses it and continues to dress, grimacing in pain as
he lifts his arms.)

ANYA

My poor little cricket. You must be in such pain.

YOUNG ISAAC

Pain? After being with you, nothing hurts.
I feel pure and holy. I'm healed! You heal me.

(He grabs her, kisses her.)

You can treat me for all my cuts and bruises. And then…
then we can make love again. No one hears
or sees us. It's like we are in our own country.

(He puts on his shirt and jacket, then puts on his Russian hat with the
flaps.)

ANYA

We must be careful.

(He embraces her. She strokes his face lovingly, touches the old scar on the
side of his forehead.)

This scar on your head is old. You came to us with it. But you never talk about it.

YOUNG ISAAC

Nothing about me. I want to know everything about you.

ANYA

Sergei, sweet, I don't know when we can be together like this again.

YOUNG ISAAC

What are you telling me?

ANYA

It's Wasic. He's your friend, isn't he?

YOUNG ISAAC

He volunteered after my good friend Pietka was accidentally killed. Wasic is supposed to join me as my new partner the next time I go after a train. I'll try and make sure he just watches the first time, a good ways from the tracks while I secure the
dynamite and set the fuse.

ANYA

Why worry about saving his skin?
What about yours?

YOUNG ISAAC

It's the way I want it after Pietka died.

ANYA

Well, you have to know that the new Commander, Major Kolpac, has taken Wasic's woman, Soya, from him.

YOUNG ISAAC

Just like that?

ANYA

Call it chain of command or military privilege. Wasic thinks he can now claim me as his woman.

YOUNG ISAAC
> I'll talk to him.

ANYA
> Shhh. Let me fight for myself. If he thinks I'm just property without feelings, he'll be disappointed. I will not be anyone's property. Yours, Wasic's, the Major's.

YOUNG ISAAC
> Wasic's a fool. He's just a hot head.

ANYA
> We have to be very careful. He's always drinking. He can get wild. You know that.

YOUNG ISAAC
> I can take care of myself. And I can take care of you as well.

ANYA
> Don't worry about me. I can take care of myself. With this, If necessary.

(Slaps her rifle.)

YOUNG ISAAC
> (Laughs.)
>
> You are something, but I still don't know a thing about you.

ANYA
> First tell me again. About your house.

YOUNG ISAAC
> My house?

ANYA
> In Georgia near Mount Kazbek. You started to tell me last time in the dugout when I was dressing your wounds.

YOUNG ISAAC
(Awkward. Uneasy.)

Oh. Yes.

ANYA

With the gilded mirrors and all those wonderful rooms
and how you and your brother could speak and read so
many languages. I forgot how many?

YOUNG ISAAC

Borders changed so often, my father thought it best that
we learn as many languages as possible. So I can read
and speak High German, low Polish, a bit of English,
Ukrainian and, of course, Russian.

ANYA

Of course. Our mother language. Such culture with your
family. So many books, so many rooms.

YOUNG ISAAC
(Uneasy)

Many rooms…Yes.

ANYA

And the silk tapestry and velvet sofas…

YOUNG ISAAC

All that, yes.

ANYA

I can hardly imagine how wonderful it must have been
for you growing up. Living almost like it was in the old
days before the Revolution. Almost like you were one of
the Romanoffs or a Russian prince.

YOUNG ISAAC

Not quite, but, wonderful yes…For a time.

ANYA

I grew up in dust and clay, eating what little we could
grow in that awful dirt in the plains near Kyev. It's true!

Nothing grew but cabbages and carrots.

YOUNG ISAAC
That is all behind us. When the war is over, we are not
going back. We're going forward to a new
country, to new lives.

ANYA
America?

YOUNG ISAAC
(confidently.)
America.

ISAAC (TO AUDIENCE)
(In unison with Young Isaac, but spoken poignantly with a sense of loss.)
America.

ANYA
Oh, I would do anything…

YOUNG ISAAC
We must not think of what we left behind.

ANYA
It's just too hard right now to forget. I still can't sleep
most nights without dreaming of my father, coming
at my mother with his fists after drowning himself in
Vodka at the tavern. She'd run out the door, leaving me
alone with him. I was only five!

YOUNG ISAAC
No more nightmares. Some things we have to learn to
forget. If we can.

ISAAC
If we can.

ANYA
I'd hide in some corner, crying, terrified, but he would
me and take up in his arms, then sit on the edge of his
bed and start crying himself, asking me to forgive him

for his anger. He would blame it first on the failure of his crops, then on my mother, then on the government and finally in the end he would curse the local Priest and the Lord Almighty for failing him, then beg my forgiveness for taking the Lord's name in vain.

YOUNG ISAAC

You were five. How could you understand…?

ANYA

I would kiss him out of fear and he would believe I forgave him….The next morning Mother would come back and he would leave, sometimes for days. And Mother would look at me like I was the reason for her pain and her loneliness.

YOUNG ISAAC

It will be different for us.

ANYA

That's why, that's the only reason why…I married.

YOUNG ISAAC

So you were married! I knew it was more than just a nasty rumor.

ANYA

No. It's true. When I first saw my husband,
Khludov, I was training to be a nurse in a Kyev
clinic. I thought he was some unusual official high up in the party. His collars were always perfectly starched and he wore this carefully groomed,
heavily waxed mustache.

YOUNG ISAAC

He sounds awful, Anya.

ANYA

I just thought he was different. But I realized soon enough he was just a drab postal clerk who expected me to wait hand and foot on him at home.

YOUNG ISAAC
Poor Anya.

ANYA
Thank God for the war. I know that sounds awful but he
was conscripted and they made him shave his moustache
and throw away his starched collar. When I was told he
was killed on his first day of combat, I cried for a day.
And that was it. Now I feel reborn.
(He kisses her.)

YOUNG ISAAC
We are both reborn, together.

ANYA
But your life was so different. I should have met you
first. With such a wonderfully cultured mother and
father. Music and books all around you.

YOUNG ISAAC
Yes.
(Suddenly he is caught up in a tormenting memory.)

ISAAC (IN YIDDISH)
Yes.

ANYA
I don't know what it feels like to be cultured. Tell me
again. What's wrong, Sergei?

YOUNG ISAAC
We should get back to camp. It's getting dark.

ANYA
You're right.

YOUNG ISAAC
(Stops)
No. There's something else.

ANYA
What.

YOUNG ISAAC

No one knows. No one can know.

ANYA

What are you saying? About us?
Don't worry about Wasic.

YOUNG ISAAC

Something else. The truth.

ANYA

About...?

YOUNG ISAAC

Anya, I should have told you before...before we
became this close. If anyone finds out, there are some in
the camp who would throw me to the wolves.

ANYA

What are we talking about? Finds out about what?
(Pause)

YOUNG ISAAC

I am not Sergei.

ANYA
(She laughs.)

Of course you are. There's not another Sergei in the
whole brigade.

YOUNG ISAAC

I'm not Sergei and I'm not Russian and I don't come
from some fancy home in Georgia.

ANYA

I see. So, you're not Sergei and you're not Russian and
you don't come from a fancy home in Georgia. Then who
made love to me? Who did I make love to? Who am I
talking to?

YOUNG ISAAC

I'm…Isaac. Lived in a modest house. Father was a tanner of skins. No silk tapestry. No velvet sofas.

ANYA

Who?

YOUNG ISAAC

Isaac Hochman. From Rovno, Poland.

ANYA

Isaac…Hochman?

YOUNG ISAAC

Yes. I'm a Jew from Poland.

ANYA

A Jew?

YOUNG ISAAC

Yes. My dear mother and father and the rest of my family were shot in one night by the Einsatzgruppen squads in the Sosenki woods near Rovno.
(Anya does not respond.)
All my friends, almost all the Jews in Rovno died with them. In one night. Thousands and thousands were stripped, shot and dumped by the Nazis into a ditch…

ANYA

Then why aren't you dead?

YOUNG ISAAC

I don't know why. Maybe after a whole day of killing, one of them just got tired and careless when it came to shooting me. Why me?

ISAAC (IN YIDDISH)
(Standing, leaning on cane, repeats what torments him.)
Why me? Why just me?
(Lights fade on old Isaac.)

YOUNG ISAAC

Why not my family? The bullet just grazed me. I was unconscious for many hours. When I woke up I was naked in the ditch. My mother and father on top of me, dead.

ANYA

No.

YOUNG ISAAC

We were all white, powdery white. Like it had snowed. But it didn't feel like snow. They had covered all of us with quicklime. They didn't even bother to bury us. And I climbed out, just like that. Half dead, naked in the middle of the Sosenki woods near Rovno.

ANYA

The scar on your forehead. Is that from…?

YOUNG ISAAC

Yes. It makes no sense, does it?
(Young Isaac grabs Anya's arm.)
Say something, Anya. I'll understand.
(Anya gently removes Young Isaac's hand from her arm. She picks up her rifle. Straps it across her shoulder.)
I lied to stay alive. Some of the men in the Brigade, like Wasic, if they knew I was a Jew, would wish me dead. But I can't lie to you anymore. Do you understand? I want you to understand. Do you? Say something.
(Lights up on Old Isaac in his nursing home bed. He sits up suddenly, confused, staring into space.)
(Anya puts on her military cap. She turns away and exits.)
(Young Isaac cries out.)
Anya!

ISAAC
(Old Isaac cries out.)
Anya!
(Lights dim on Young Isaac standing alone.)
(Lights up on Anna reading. She clutches the pages close to her, clearly moved by what She has read, and she whispers through her sadness.)

ANNA
(Whispers sadly in English to herself.)
No. No.

ISAAC
(Whispering.)
No!
YOUNG ISAAC (IN RUSSIAN)
Don't go, Anya.
(Lights fade on Young Isaac.)
(Isaac throws off the covers and starts to get out of bed.
He reaches for his coat, falters, almost loses his balance.
Sits back down on the bed.)
(Mercedes rushes in. He looks at her. Begins to realize where he is.)

ISAAC
Not you.
(He falls back on the bed. Speaks a garble of Polish and Russian.)
Niey. Nyet. Nish du.
(Mercedes covers him gently, kindly, trying to be comforting.)

(LIGHTS FADE ON ISAAC, MERCEDES AND ANNA.)

SCENE FIVE

(Isaac's apartment. Light up on Anna. She is sitting at a kitchen table looking through Isaac's cloth satchel. She places his cane near her chair. Broken doorbell buzzes weakly. Anna continues to look through the satchel, pulling out old photographs and Isaac's hand-written pages. She starts to read them when the doorbell buzzes again, followed by heavy knocking.)
(The scene is in English.)

ANNA

Who is it?

JOSEF (O.S.)

**Who is it? It's me! Your brother Josef!
Do you remember your brother?**

ANNA

It's open. Just jiggle the knob.
(Sound of jiggling.)

JOSEF

Crap!
(Josef, 34, enters. He is dressed in a dark overcoat wearing a custom-made suit underneath.)
Do you remember anything?

ANNA

What?

JOSEF

Do you remember who I am? Where you live? Why you're hanging out in some old man's apartment?

ANNA

Yes. Yes. And yes! I'm here gathering up some things to bring to Isaac.
(Holds up cane.)

Like this. He told me it was the first real purchase he made in America. Reminded him of the one his Grandfather owned.

JOSEF

So now you're in the cane shipping business.

ANNA

You don't understand.

JOSEF

What don't I understand? You took this Isaac to a Nursing Home where he belongs. That's enough.

ANNA

If you just took time to read his accounts.

JOSEF

Do you remember you were supposed to meet Louis and me tonight at that wine bar downtown?

ANNA

I must have forgotten.

JOSEF

He wanted to show you that new apartment building where you should be living. Not in this cruddy place.

ANNA

This is our building. You grew up here.

JOSEF

It was an antique then and it's a rent-controlled relic now. I'll pay whatever it costs. I just want you out of here!

ANNA

Did you know when Mother was dying, Isaac would come by and ask if there was anything she needed. You didn't know that, did you?

JOSEF

What are you saying? I wasn't around for Mother? I told you a hundred times I was traveling all over, making money, building a future for all of us.

ANNA

You're not listening.

JOSEF

I came by to see Mother many times. I tried to get her the best of care but she refused to leave.

ANNA

You had your priorities. I had mine. Only Mother ran out of priorities.

JOSEF

Jesus, Anna, stop living in the past. You're only 27 and you got your whole life ahead of you.

ANNA

I'm 29.

JOSEF

Still too young.

ANNA

We're different creatures, Josef. All I can think about right now is how poor Isaac feels.

JOSEF

I don't give a damn.

ANNA

Don't you remember when you were still a young boy how he'd always greet you in the hallway with a smile and lift you way high in his arms so you touch the ceiling?

JOSEF

That was a long time ago. Can't remember one old Russian from another. Halls were full of them.

ANNA

> Isaac is Polish. He's a Polish Jew.

JOSEF

> Poland, Russia, a Jew from Timbuktu. What the hell does it matter? He's yesterday's news.

ANNA

> There's so much in these pages of Isaac's. How his whole family was murdered in one night by the Nazis…

JOSEF

> He's a whining old pain in the butt. Sick and old. There's nothing more you can do for him.
> (Under his breath.)
> Scheisse.

ANNA

> I remember our father cursing like that. Good thing he took off before Isaac moved in across the hall. If Isaac had ever heard Father cursing like that…

JOSEF

> Scheisse is a fine German curse.
> (Anna shakes her head, exasperated.)
> It's our heritage! It's Beethoven and Bach and Goethe! We're German-Americans, damn it! It has nothing to do with that ugly war! And nothing to do with that old man's war either!

ANNA

> Did it ever bother you that we never knew one thing about Father during the war? He was a young man in Germany then. Old enough to fight.

JOSEF

> So what if he fought? He was no different than millions of young Americans conscripted and sent off to fight for their country. When it was over, he came to America and married Mother. That's it! Was is war. When it's over, you want to forget it.

ANNA

Isaac doesn't want us to forget.

JOSEF

His war has nothing to do with us.

ANNA

Maybe. Did you ever wonder why Father changed his name from Braunau to Brown?

JOSEF

What's your point? Millions come over and change their name. To sound more American.

ANNA

Isaac told me all about Braunau.

JOSEF

Did he? Well, Father told me long before that old fart of yours started infecting your brain. Braunau was Hitler's old village where he was born. So there! Father knew all about it. That was another good reason why he changed it as quickly as he could. He was no fool.

ANNA

So you always knew.

JOSEF

Knew what? So he changed his family name. That's the long and short of it. What's got into you? You've got to stop all this nonsense about Father!

ANNA

When he walked out…when he turned his back on all of us so suddenly…just when Mother was weakest and needed him most.

JOSEF

I don't want to hear anymore.

ANNA

He just vanished like that.

(She snaps her fingers.)

Like he didn't give a damn about us!

JOSEF

You were barely seven when he left. Too young to understand anything.

ANNA

I was ten…going on twenty.

JOSEF

They drifted apart. Simple as that. Marriages fail.
Even German-American marriages fail. What's the
point!? He was a good man, Anna! In his way.

ANNA
(Bitterly.)

In his way? Really? I never told you about the letter
Mother received just before she died.

JOSEF

A letter? From Father?

ANNA

I've tried to put it out of my mind.

JOSEF

What was in it?

ANNA

I came home and found Mother sitting up in her bed,
sobbing and choking back her tears. And there on her
blanket was what was left of the letter and the envelope.
She had ripped them up into little pieces.

JOSEF

Why would she…?

ANNA

I don't know why. She never told me anything. Just
pointed at the pieces and told me to gather them up and
put them in a paper bag. I stuffed all the pieces in a bag

while she watched me so intently and when I finished, she gripped my arm with all the strength left in her and told me to burn it good. Burn it good, she kept repeating. And I did. I went out in the hall, dumped the bag with all the pieces in the incinerator and burned it good.

JOSEF

That's it?

ANNA

I keep thinking about it.

JOSEF

About what?

ANNA

Why Mother got so furious. She found strength enough to destroy the letter.

JOSEF

So it ended up being nothing but ashes.

ANNA

It could have been from him.

JOSEF

What are you saying?

ANNA

Or maybe it was about him, from someone else, some government agency, some group searching for him. Maybe it was Father himself confessing to something unspeakable.

JOSEF

Christ Almighty! What has that old man done to your brain?

ANNA

It could have been sent from anywhere. Germany, South America, Israel, anywhere!

JOSEF

Stop it! You're making yourself crazy! You burnt some letter for Mother. That's the end of it!

ANNA

You're right. I burnt it for Mother and she died a week later without once mentioning the letter again. Whatever was in it, she didn't want us to know about it.

JOSEF

So it's over and done with. No more! It's only you we have to worry about now, Anna. You've got to think about your future. Seriously. You're barely making a living and you dress like some indigent drop-out from a hick college. You're a beautiful woman under all those rags you wear.

ANNA

I'll be fine.
(She takes a breath, collects herself.)
I start a new job in a month at a pre-school by Columbia. I replace a teacher who's getting married.

JOSEF

I've introduced you to some fine young men in the past. You go out with them once and they never hear from you again.

ANNA

If you like them so much, why don't you call them?

JOSEF

Funny.
(Anna starts gathering Isaac's pages.)
What are you doing?

ANNA

Putting Isaac back in order.

JOSEF

Stop fussing over that nonsense.

ANNA

It's not nonsense, Josef. Here.
(She hands him some pages.)
You'll see it's not nonsense.

JOSEF

What's with you, Anna? Enough with him!
(He throws pages to the floor.)
(Anna kneels to gather up pages. Josef, realizing he overreacted, kneels
down to help. Anna waves him away.)

ANNA

You've made your point. Go.

JOSEF

I didn't mean to…Are you alright?

ANNA

I'm fine. Everything is fine. Go.
(She gets up with the pages, sits at the table and starts putting them back
in order.)

JOSEF

I don't know what got into me. I'm sorry. Here.
(Takes out a wad of money and tried to hand it to her.)
To cover your expenses for the next few days.

ANNA

I don't want it!

JOSEF

Give me a break, Anna! It's almost Christmas.

ANNA

I don't care. Please. Go!

JOSEF

Then leave it for Isaac.

ANNA

What is it? Blood money? No!

(Anna angrily pushes away his hand clutching the money, then continues to sort through Isaac's pages.)

JOSEF
(Shakes his head in exasperation and kisses her on the cheek.)
This Sunday. Remember. Louis and I will pick you up in your apartment. Please don't forget. Love you.
(He starts to exit, hesitates and slips money under a pile of Isaac's papers on the table without Anna seeing it.)
(Anna is upset. She looks at the yellow pages she was holding.
Lights fade.)
(Music begins. Projection of Isaac's yellow handwritten pages slowly dissolving one into the other.)
(She begins to read Isaac's words.)
(Lights up on Old Isaac at the side of the stage, dressed in his long coat and mouton cap, sitting on a stool, his cane across his lap. He speaks his words to the audience.)

ISAAC
When I came home from school, I saw that my father's millstones had stopped turning. I knew then the war had finally come to Rovno. Soon, very soon after, I saw my brother, Sol, and his wife Lyuba, for the very last time.
(Lights fade out on Anna.)
(Isaac remains on a stool, speaking what he was written,
as he remembers and relives the scene.)

SCENE SIX

(Lights up on a young Isaac. No scar on his forehead. He carries a satchel like Old Isaac's over his shoulder.)
(Cross fade as Music and Projections of pages fade out.)
(He pauses, listening to the sound of an approaching German army. Flashes of red from distant explosions.)
(The sound of war planes, tanks and machine guns echo in and out of the scene.)
(Lights up on Isaac's father Lazar. He wears a leather tanning apron and leather cap.)
(They speak in Yiddish.)

LAZAR

I want to bring your brother and Lyuba back home as soon as possible, son.

YOUNG ISAAC

Is it war, father? I saw smoke and heard planes just over the hills near Rovno.

LAZAR

Just go to Sol's clinic and tell him and Lyuba, I want them home this instant.

YOUNG ISAAC

But Sol will be busy with his patients. Why rush him?

ISAAC (AS LAZAR.)

Just go, Isaac. Sol will understand.

YOUNG ISAAC

Understand what?

LAZAR
(Embraces him.)

Don't you worry, son. I just want all of us together for Shabbos.

YOUNG ISAAC

It's too early to eat. Mother hasn't even begun cooking.

LAZAR

No more.

YOUNG ISAAC

Is it the Germans? Are they here already?

LAZAR

Isaac, we're going to be fine. If they get here, if the Germans get here, what can happen? If they take away our tanning plant, we have our land. If they take away our land, we have our house. If they take our house, we have our money; if they take our money, we still have our family, son, and together we will start over somewhere else. Go. I want us all to be together for Shabbos.

(Lights fade on Lazar.)

ISAAC (IN YIDDISH)
(Echoing painfully his father's words.)

Together…we still have our family…we will start over… somewhere…somewhere…together.

(Lights up on young Isaac talking to Sol and Lyuba in his clinic. Lyuba, 25, is dressed in a white nurse's uniform. Sol, 27, also is dressed in a white gown with a stethoscope around his neck.)
(They speak in Yiddish.)

YOUNG ISAAC

Sol, Lyuba, Father said you should both come home with me, right now. Quickly as possible. For certain, Sol. That's what he said.

SOL

Izz, do you see all the patients waiting outside?

YOUNG ISAAC

I didn't look. I don't want to look. We have to hurry. I heard the sound of machine guns on the way here. Close by. Strange. They remind me of how wet wood crack- les in our fireplace. That's where we all should be. By

our fireplace. Father wants us all together for Shabbos.
Make him hurry, Lyuba.

LYUBA
> Shhh. Go upstairs, sweetie, to the library. I know you
> won't have any trouble finding something to read. When
> Sol is finished, we'll all go home together and enjoy a
> wonderful Shabbos meal.

(Sudden commotion. Harsh voice heard, barking sharp orders,
"Raus! Alle! Raus!" Raus!")

SOL
(Grabs Isaac.)
> Hide. Quickly.

YOUNG ISAAC
> Why…?

SOL
(To Lyuba)
> Hide him! Quickly. Upstairs. In the library.

(Lyuba leads Isaac offstage, kissing him before he exits, then turns just as
Einsatzgruppen Commandant Bichel enters.)
(Their dialogue is in German.)

COMMANDANT
(He is wearing a dark brown uniform with leather straps, tan cap, carrying
a pair of leather gloves in his hand.)
(Sol and Commandant speak German.)
> You will attend immediately to my wounded.

SOL (IN GERMAN.)
> Of course. I'll just tell my patients outside, I'll see them
> as soon as I can.

COMMANDANT
> You have no patients. They have been removed.

SOL
> You had no authority to…

COMMANDANT

I am the only authority!

SOL

I insist on carrying out my medical duties as I see fit.
(At that, the Commandant slaps Sol hard across the face with one of his
loose gloves. Sol is stunned. Old Isaac, as if experiencing the blow himself,
stands up, stunned as well.)
(Lyuba is startled and rushes to his side.)
(Young Isaac watches from above through a half-open door. Lights
brighten on Old Isaac as he speaks in English, reliving every second.)

ISAAC (TO AUDIENCE)

I had never seen my brother treated with anything but
reverence and respect. I shuddered inside, afraid to utter
a sound, watching it all in secret through the library
door. It didn't seem real. I turned away for a moment,
sick, frightened. The sanctity of my brother's world had
been violated.
(Dialogue between Commandant and Sol continues in German.)

COMMANDANT

Now I will tell you what your duties are. Some of my
troops need immediate transfusions. You will round up
the youngest children in the town and draw blood from
them!

SOL

Children? You want me to take blood from children?

COMMANDANT

From infants, Jewish infants, first.

SOL

From infants? From babies? It will kill them.

COMMANDANT

I don't want to weaken the able-bodied men in town. We
will need them to work for us immediately so begin now
to round up all the children and especially all the babies.

SOL

I will find you healthy young volunteers and gladly treat your men.

COMMANDANT

You will not touch my soldiers! A German doctor will care for the German wounded. Your job will be to draw blood only, and only from the very young children and babies. Now!

SOL

I cannot! It will be criminal. No doctor in all conscience would agree to such…

COMMANDANT

One last time, pig! I order you.
(He unsnaps his side holster and draws his pistol.)

SOL
(He speaks in German.)

…In all conscience, I am still a doctor…

LYUBA
(Speaking in Yiddish.)

Sol! Don't!
(The Commandant shoots Sol directly in his forehead without a moment's hesitation. Sol's head jerks backward and he falls, dead.)
(Lyuba screams, runs at the Commandant in a fury and the Commandant just as swiftly swiftly shoots her.)

COMMANDANT
(In disgust, looking at the dead bodies before him.
He turns and shouts an order in German to soldiers outside.)

Burn this place! It's useless.
(Lights slowly fade on scene. Sound of smashing windows and crackle of fire.)
(Then silence.)
(Lights up on Anna. She has been moved to tears.)
(We see projection of Isaac's pages. Then old Isaac, still standing in a dim light, sits down, exhausted by the memory, speaking his handwritten words to the audience.)

ISAAC

I wanted to scream. I wanted to grieve and cry out, "No! Wild beasts!" But I held back out of fear, out of panic. I couldn't move, but I knew I had to escape. I saw the soldiers rushing in with pitch-tar torches, smashing windows, kicking down doors. It was then I ran to the back of the library, squeezed through the window and slid down the sloping back-roof. And I ran, ran without looking back. Ran with my eyes flooded with tears. Ran back to my home, to my family's home, without Sol and Lyuba. Gone. Forever.

ISAAC (CONTINUING; IN YIDDISH)

Nito Ayoyfeybik.

(Lights fade on Old Isaac.)

(Anna puts down Isaac's pages.)

(Page projections fade out.)

(Anna is emotionally spent. Finally, she stands, gathers scattered papers from the table and sees Josef's money underneath it. She ignores it at first and puts pages in the satchel. She picks up Isaac's cane. Starts to leave. Then she studies Josef's money money on the table. She touches it, starts to leave again without it, then takes it and puts it in Isaac's satchel.)

(Lights dim on table.)

SCENE SEVEN

(Lights up on Isaac's bed in the Nursing Home. Isaac is half asleep, half remembering. Repeating over and over in English and Yiddish in a whisper just before he dreams.)

ISAAC

Meyn Bruder! Toyt. Toyt. Ale! Everyone! Toyt. No. No!
(Lights dim. He sits up in bed. He will watch, remember and relive the scenes that follow.)
(Lights up on Young Isaac, wearing a Mouton cap, standing with a small suitcase and satchel over his shoulder. Other suitcases and bundles at his feet belong to other family members. His Grandfather's cane, with an elegant brass handle, rests on one of the bundles.)
(Kcholp, a 26-year old Polish fireman, enters, wearing a fireman's rubber coat.)
(They speak in Polish.)

YOUNG ISAAC

Kcholp, what are you doing here? There's no fire.

KCHOLP

Are you leaving yet?

YOUNG ISAAC

We're not going far?

KCHOLP

Really? I heard different from my policeman cousin in town.

YOUNG ISAAC

What would he know about us?

KCHOLP

The Einsatzgruppen put him in a new police battalion and he heard that all you Jews in Rovno will be traveling a good distance east for, what did he call it…yes… resettlement.

YOUNG ISAAC

It's not any concern of yours.

KCHOLP

Tell your father…

YOUNG ISAAC

He's busy packing. We're allowed only six kilos each.
And my Aunt Frieda is too weak to pack for herself.

KCHOLP

I see. Six kilos? Not much. All the rest you know will
belong to the Schutzstaffel. The SS will take everything
you leave behind. Your father knows what's coming.

YOUNG ISAAC

Not true. This is just a temporary…

KCHOLP

Look, my wife and I love that gilded mirror in the
hallway and those watercolors of wildflowers you have
hanging in your father's study…

YOUNG ISAAC

Get out!

KCHOLP

Wouldn't you rather give some of your precious possessions to a friend and neighbor than to strangers?

YOUNG ISAAC

We are not leaving for good. We have no intention of
selling anything in our house.

KCHOLP

Sell? You don't have any time left to see anything. You'll
be gone by tomorrow. So why don't you ask your father if
he would like to give away some of his precious belongings to friends while he can. Like that expensive cane.
You won't be needing it.

YOUNG ISAAC

My Grandfather's cane? Who do you think you are? My Grandfather gave it to me just before he died. It belongs to me, to my family. Everything belongs to my family!

KCHOLP

Not for long. It's quite an impressive cane. May I?
(He tries to pick it up. Isaac pushes him away and picks up cane himself.)

YOUNG ISAAC

Get out! You're no friend. You're a vulture, that's what! You want to see this cane? Here! Here!
(Swings cane at his head.)
Get out. Now!

KCHOLP
(Arrogant and angry.)

You fool. Such nerve. With your father smelling up the land all around with his filthy skins and hides. That's why you have no neighbors. Who can stand that stink? We all had to get far enough away from that God-awful stink. That Jewish stink.

YOUNG ISAAC

You bastard! It has nothing to do with…

KCHOLP

I know what happened to your doctor brother and his wife. Everyone knows. Don't you understand? Are you all blind to what's happening? Before the week is out, someone else, maybe even me, will be living in this house and you and your family won't matter anymore and none of you will be any better off than your brother.

YOUNG ISAAC

What are you saying?

KCHOLP

Do you know what my cousin was doing all last week?

YOUNG ISAAC

What do you mean we won't matter? What has my brother's murder to do with…

KCHOLP

My cousin's battalion has been digging a trench in the Sosenki forest near Kostopol…Almost a kilometer long. Deep. Long and deep enough to bury a good ten thousand of you. That's what he said.

YOUNG ISAAC

You don't know what you're talking about, you shit!

KCHOLP

You'll see. You'll see soon enough.

YOUNG ISAAC

Get out!

KCHOLP

Tell your father he's no big shot anymore. You're nothing. You're all nothing! Good riddance to your face and your stink.

(Young Isaac swings cane at Kcholp, hitting his shoulder. Kcholp laughs, spits at him.)

Go to hell. That's where all you Jews belong!

(Young Isaac stands there, full of fury, shouting at him as Kcholp exits.)

YOUNG ISAAC

If you take anything from our house while we're away, anything, a spoon, a plate, a cup, a mirror, I swear I will break into your house, beat the stuffing out of you and take back everything that is ours. It is ours. Ours alone. It will always be ours!

(Lights fade on Young Isaac.)
(Old Isaac is agitated by what he remembers.)
(Sound of warplanes, gunshots, marching boots.)
(Sound of a harsh whistle. The shouting of German orders to "mach schnell!")
(Lights up on Young Isaac. He picks up his suitcase and satchel. He tries to pack his Grandfather's cane into his satchel but there is no room. He kisses

it, puts it on the floor carefully, lovingly, leaving it behind.)
(He turns back to the audience, walking upstage.)
(There is wild impression of harsh whistles, wheeling flashlights and the shrill voice of a German soldier shouting orders to put down belongings and strip.)

NAZI VOICES (O.S.)
Ausziehen! Strippen. Mach schnell!
(Young Isaac strips, turns, faces audience. The trench must be imagined in front of him just beyond the stage.)
(A Commandant appears behind Isaac with Kcholp's cousin, a newly-appointed policeman, wearing a police cap and a poorly fitting jacket. He follows the Commandant slavishly.)
(Off stage sound of weeping and different voices reciting the Kaddish.)
(Pinspot on Old Isaac's face as he recites the Kaddish along with the offstage voices.)
(Commandant orders the policemen to start shooting them.)

COMMANDANT (IN GERMAN.)
Schieben! Toten…Alle. Schieben!

YOUNG ISAAC
(Crying out in despair in Polish to the Polish policeman he recognizes.)
I know you! You're Kcholp's cousin. Please! Shoot me first. Before my family. Shoot me first. I'm ready. I don't want to see them die. Shoot me.

COMMANDANT
(Shouting angrily in Polish at the policeman.)
Shoot him…Now!
(Isaac rushes the policeman who aims in panic and just grazes Isaac's forehead. Isaac touches his forehead which is suddenly bloody and he sinks to the ground unconscious.)
(Lights fade on Young Isaac.) (Sound of Kaddish fades.)
(Lights bang up on Isaac's bed. Isaac is in great turmoil.)
(He throws off covers. It is as if he is struggling to get out of the deep grave with his family's bodies pressing down on him.)
(He flails his arms, climbs out of bed, knocking over the side table.)

ISAAC
(Crying out in grief in English and Yiddish.)
Mameh! Tateh! Vilde Khius! Beasts!

(Mercedes rushes in and tries to restrain him, but he swings at her and pushes her aside. She falls to the floor.)

MERCEDES
(She screams.)
Security! Security!
(A tall orderly rushes in. He grabs Isaac. Tries to restrain him. Isaac struggles, fighting back, still confused. He faces the orderly, looks at him. Thinks he's Kcholp.)

ISAAC
(Speaking Polish.)
You? Kcholp? Nyet! Kill me. Not them! No! Me!
(Orderly takes down Isaac, pinning him to the ground. Mercedes motions to Orderly not to hurt Isaac, then rushes out and comes back with a syringe and injects Isaac with some strong sedative.)
(Isaac whispers in both English and Yiddish in his groggy state.)
What? Vos? Anya? Kumm tsu mir…
(Then to audience.)
Kumm tsu mir…Kum tsu mir
(Isaac looks at audience, freezes. Music comes in, then fades.)
(Lights fade.)

END OF ACT ONE

ACT TWO

SCENE EIGHT

(In the dark, we hear phone ringing.)
(Lights up dimly on Isaac's bed in the nursing home.
Isaac stirs, mumbles something in a garble of language.
Mercedes, wary of another outburst, holds another syringe in her
hand. When Isaac twists and turns, she quickly administers another
sedative shot. She watches Isaac's body relax.)
(She exits.)
(Lights up on Anna appearing outside Isaac's room.
She has brought his satchel with the old map inside
and the cane. Mercedes sees her, puts her finger
to her lips signaling quiet.)
(They speak in English.)

MERCEDES

He's resting finally.

ANNA

Not upstairs? Not in lockdown?

MERCEDES

I told you I would tell you before a decision is made. It
hasn't been made yet.
(Looking at what she is carrying.)
Are you planning some kind of trip?
(Sees cane.)
Not with Isaac, I hope. He's in no condition.

ANNA

No. No. Thanks for calling about the incident. I know he
can get quite emotional…I'm sorry he was so upset with
you.

MERCEDES

I don't know what set him off. Something terrible. We
had to sedate him before he hurt himself. I'm sorry.

ANNA

> I never saw him that way. Maybe these small possessions of his might calm him.

MERCEDES

> I'm afraid the cane could become a lethal weapon in his hand.

ANNA

> But it reminds him of his Zayda.

MERCEDES
(Puzzled)

> Zayda? What's his Zayda?

ANNA
(Smiles)

> His Grandfather.

MERCEDES

> Ahhh. I understand. His abuelo. His Grandfather. So that's his Grandfather's cane.

ANNA

> Yes. He bought it in this country because it reminded him of his home, his family.

MERCEDES

> And his abuelo.

(Anna nods, smiling in agreement.)
(Anna goes to the door, holding the satchel and cane. Mercedes stops her.)

> No. Isaac shouldn't be disturbed. He's in a precarious state. Let him rest.

ANNA

> You're not planning to move him upstairs?

MERCEDES

> I know how you feel, Miss Brown…

ANNA

Anna.

MERCEDES

But there's nothing I can do, Anna, if the administration decides that Mr. Hochman is a constant danger to himself or…others.

ANNA

Please…

MERCEDES

I understand. I will do everything in my power.

ANNA

May I see him?

MERCEDES

It's way past visiting hours. We don't want to disturb the other residents. Leave the souvenirs with me and I will make sure.

ANNA

They're not souvenirs! They're part of his life. Part of his memories. I'll hold on to them.

MERCEDES

Please don't leave the cane with him.

ANNA

I won't. But I will wait here until he awakes.

MERCEDES

If you need me…
(She hugs Anna.)

ANNA

I'll be fine.
(Mercedes brings Anna a chair. Anna grips Mercedes' hand and sits. Mercedes smiles, then exits.)
(Anna sits with satchel and cane across her lap, waiting. Distant sound

of coughing from other residents. Some moaning. Anna, restless, pulls out
pages from from the satchel and reads more of Isaac's life.)
(Music fades in with the projection of Isaac's pages slowly turning.)
(Lights up on old Isaac at the side of the stage in his long coat and mouton cap, lean leaning on his cane near the wooden stool, speaking to the
audience the words written in English that Anna is reading.)
(Lights fade low on Anna eventually going out.)

ISAAC

> I was picked to blow up trains because I was the small-
> est and the quickest. My dear friend, Pietka, was not as
> small as me and not as quick, but he was picked as my
> partner because we were close. When he died, Wasic
> volunteered to work with me. It was not my choice. We
> met with a partisan named Alyosha, the Brigade's old
> hand at demolition, who had instructed dear Pietka and
> me on how to blow up trains in the past.

(Lights up on Alyosha, 46.)

> Now he had to do it all over for Wasic's sake.
> Alyosha had been injured badly many times over doing
> what he now taught us to do. His face wore the marks
> of past explosions, a notched nose, a patch over one eye,
> one pulverized ear. Looking at him always reminded us
> of the danger. But after Pietka's awful death, I did not
> need any reminders.

(Lights linger on old Isaac who watches from the side of the stage as
projection of pages slowly fade out.)
(Lights up on Young Isaac, wearing a similar mouton cap with ear flaps and
Wasic Wasic, 31. Wasic is a gruff-looking veteran. He wears a Russian army
overcoat cinched by a belt that carries a holster and a sheath containing a
hunting knife.)
(Alyosha wears a bandage over one eye and carries a bundle of dynamite in
a satch satchel with fuse and string inside. He puts satchel down at Young
Isaac's feet.)
(They speak in Russian.)

ALYOSHA

> Understand men, if you time it right, the engine and the
> boiler will explode first and the rest of the cars will derail
> and crumple down the embankment. There will be hot
> pieces of metal exploding in the air. They will burn right
> through your clothing and cut deep into your flesh. Run

far enough away and you will be safe. Typonimayesh?

YOUNG ISAAC
Da. Ponimayu!
(Alyosha waits for Wasic to respond.)

WASIC
Ponimayu!

ALYOSHA
Good! Now there will be much steam and confusion. Do not look back. These cars are coming from the Russian front and carry tanks and artillery and troops along with cattle and whatever treasures these Nazi bastards stole retreating from Mother Russia. Don't collect souvenirs. Ponimayesh?

WASIC
Da! Ponimayu!
(Alyosha does not wait for Young Isaac to respond which annoys Wasic.)

ALYOSHA
Watch your footing on the embankment. Full of gravel. When it rains it gets slick. Test your footing each time you climb to the tracks. One slip running down and I'll have to teach a new team. And I hate doing this. Ponimayesh?

YOUNG ISAAC
Da!

WASIC
Da!

ALYOSHA
Now, Wasic. Sergei here is experienced so follow him closely.

WASIC
Don't need to. Pietka showed me everything.

ALYOSHA
He did? When?

WASIC

The night before…his last time…

ALYOSHA

Showed you everything, did he? Did he tell you why he died? Did he tell you how he died? Did he tell you what not to do so you won't die?

YOUNG ISAAC

I thought Pietka was dead asleep that night before he… He never mentioned that he was with you.

(Wasic laughs.)

WASIC

That's how much you knew your so-called friend. Pietka and I spent half the night drinking that Samogon the Major Kolpack brewed for us.

YOUNG ISAAC

You got him drunk.

WASIC

I didn't twist his arm. He just loved celebrating with me.

YOUNG ISAAC

Celebrating what?

WASIC

That last train he blew. He couldn't wait to show me the steps. Taught me everything. And we drank a toast to each and every train he blew up with you.

YOUNG ISAAC

What did you think you were doing? You're the reason he was too sick to move off the tracks that day.

WASIC

I'm the reason?

YOUNG ISAAC

I just thought he had a bad night…He was tripping all

over himself. I tried to keep him away from the tracks but he wouldn't listen. Right after we set the charges, I told him to run, but he looked at me like I was speaking another language. Then he fell to his knees. I tried to drag him away with the train coming and the fuse burning. I tried, but he kept pushing me away with what little strength he had left in him. I shouted, I screamed at him to run. But he didn't move. And then I ran.

WASIC

So it was you after all.

YOUNG ISAAC

Me?

WASIC

You could have saved him, Sergei, or whatever your name is, whoever you are.

YOUNG ISAAC

I told you I tried…What do you mean, whoever I am?

WASIC

I mean you left your good friend Pietka behind to blow up along with the train. You killed him, you dirty…!
(Young Isaac jumps at Wasic. Wasic takes out a hunting knife, but Young Isaac grabs grabs the arms holding the knife and holds it down until Wasic has to drop it. At this this point Alyosha steps in. He is massively strong and separates the two, literally tossing both of them aside in different directions.)

ALYOSHA

I told you I hate breaking in a new team. If you want to kill each other, do it on your time. Not mine. Typonimayesh?
(No answer. Both men glaring at each other.)
Ponimayesh?
(Alyosha checks his watch.)
Now check your watch. The Germans run their military transports precisely on time. Are you listening, Wasic? Wasic?

WASIC
>**Da!**

ALYOSHA
>**When you both go out, there'll be no weapons. Nothing. No guns, no knives. In case you're left behind, dead or alive, we don't help these Nazi bastards to our weapons.**
(He picks up Wasic's knife.)
>**Typonimayesh?**
(Sergei nods yes.)
>**Wasic?**
(Wasic, still raging, nods yes.)
(He gives the knife back to Wasic.)
(He begins the instructions in a monotone.)
>**To prepare!**
(Old Isaac standing at the side of the stage, repeats simultaneously in Russian to the underlined phrases of Alyosha's instructions that are deeply ingrained in his memory.)
>**Tie the sticks of dynamite together. Ponimayesh, Wasic?**
(Wasic nods, still angry.)

>**Good! Insert the fuse…Notice, Wasic, the fuse is short. We have limited resources. Seal it with just a bit of soft putty. Place the bundle between the rails and the wooden ties with some of the dynamite resting on the tracks just in case the fuse fails. Light the fuse and run like hell. Run! Right, Sergei?**

YOUNG ISAAC
>**Right.**

ALYOSHA
>**Wasic?**

WASIC
(Whispers in a growl.)
>**Right!**
(Almost a sneer.)
(Lights fade on Old Isaac.)

ALYOSHA
>**Keep running. Do not turn back. Do not waste a second.**

If your partner slips, if he crumbles, if he can't move because he is sick, it's his problem, not yours. Do you understand, Wasic? It's his problem. Typonimayesh, Wasic?

WASIC
Da! Da!

ALYOSHA
(Checking his watch.)

You have exactly one hour. Please don't kill each other until you have done the job. No weapons on the job.
(Both men nod.)
(Lights fade on scene.)
(Lights brighten on Anna. She has fallen asleep. The satchel and cane slip from her hands to the floor.)

SCENE NINE

(Lights up on Isaac's bed. We hear him muttering in his sleep.)

ISAAC
(Muttering in Russian.)
  You…? Wasic?…Why…?…Why?
(Sound of an explosion and hissing steam.)
(Lights fade on Anna.)
(Old Isaac slowly gets out of bed. He looks around, puzzled, disoriented, see his overcoat and mouton cap. He looks around for his cane and satchel with the map; confused, he goes back to overcoat and cap, takes them off the hook, holds them close, then tenderly clutches them, then exhausted sits down on bed with cap and hat across his lap, trying to catch his breath.)
(Lights dim on Old Isaac. He continues to watch, remember, and relive the scene.)
(Lights up on Young Isaac.)
(Young Isaac is lying in the woods. His pants torn, his face and arms streaked with blood. He tries to rise. He falls back, rubs the back of his head. He looks at his hand. There's blood on his fingers. He closes his eyes, too weak to move.)
(Anya comes running towards him. She carries a bag with bandages and first aid ointments.) (They speak in Russian.)

ANYA
  I knew it. I know you wouldn't die on me. Tell me you're alive. Isaac…Look at me, Isaac!

YOUNG ISAAC
(Opens eyes.)
  Anya? You called me…?

ANYA
  Wasic is running around the camp telling everyone how you tried to kill him on the tracks. How he fought back and knocked you flat and how he ran from the exploding train just in time. He was sure you never got up and must have died in the explosion.

YOUNG ISAAC
I didn't...I don't remember...I'm bleeding...
(Shows her his hand, points to the back of his head.)

ANYA
(Goes behind him. Sees the open wound.)
My poor cricket. I told you to be careful, Isaac.
(She starts treating him.)

YOUNG ISAAC
Why?

ANYA
Why? I love you and it's not worth loving you if you're
dead.
(She starts treating the back of his head.)

YOUNG ISAAC
You shouted out my name. My real name.

ANYA
Oh. That.

YOUNG ISAAC
If anyone hears...

ANYA
Did you hear what I said? Wasic is going around brag-
ging how he escaped certain death at your hands.

YOUNG ISAAC
I never touched him. I lit the fuse and told him to run
and the next thing, I...felt something strike my head.

ANYA
Don't touch it. That's my job.

YOUNG ISAAC
I was in a haze, couldn't get my legs to work, so I started
to crawl away. The fuse was burning down. I heard the
train. I crawled, rolled down the embankment, managed

to get on my feet. And I ran, ran until the edge of the woods, then felt the explosion. And fell here. Blacked out. Maybe it was the explosion that did most of the damage.

ANYA

No. Simple. Wasic tried to kill you.

YOUNG ISAAC

I can't believe…

ANYA

(Kisses the top of his head.)

It was Wasic. Not an explosion. Wasic, the worm. With something heavy. Probably a rock.

YOUNG ISAAC

I didn't see him pick up anything.

ANYA

You had your back to him, doing your job while he was doing his.

YOUNG ISAAC

He's a good soldier. He wouldn't…

(She continues to treat his wound behind him.)

ANYA

Did you know, the night before he joined you, he tried to drag me off to his bedroll, claiming me for his own? I warned you he would. He swore if you got near me again, he would kill you.

YOUNG ISAAC

Did you sleep with…?

ANYA

You know me better than that. I shove my rifle point blank in his face and threatened to blow off his hot head. He backed off. So did I.

(Isaac smiles, tried to turn and kiss her, but she stops him.)

Don't move, you idiot. I still have some patching up to do.

YOUNG ISAAC

Maybe you're right. Maybe it was Wasic.

ANYA

I think I will blow his head off the next time I see him.
Hold still.

YOUNG ISAAC

He really thinks I'm dead?

ANYA

He wants to believe…He told Major Kolpak the
Brigade is better off without you. Told everyone your
real name. Been shouting "Isaac" all over the camp.
Pietka must have told him everything.

YOUNG ISAAC

That bastard got Pietka drunk! That's why.

ANYA

A slimy worm. That's all he is!

YOUNG ISAAC

So, it's all out in the open. Why are you here, Anya?
I'm a marked man.

ANYA

I know who you really are. I know what I feel. Let Wasic
blubber on. Makes no difference to me.

YOUNG ISAAC

He told the Major all this?

ANYA

Told anyone who would listen.

YOUNG ISAAC

Then…then it's all over for me. You should stay away. I
don't want you to get hurt.

ANYA

I'm used to being with men who are total disasters.

Don't you understand? I love you whether you are Sergei
or Isaac. But no more lying.

YOUNG ISAAC
(Anya presses too hard on his wound and Isaac yells in pain.)
Owwwwwe! No more…

ANYA
Lying?

YOUNG ISAAC
No more.

ANYA
The Major told me he practically kicked Wasic out of his
headquarters when that Wasic bastard turned on you.

YOUNG ISAAC
The Major did that?

ANYA
The Major made it clear to everyone. "We are fighting
the Nazi, not the Jews." He told the whole camp. "We
need all the good soldiers we can muster. Isaac or Sergei,
who gives a shit, as long as he pulls his own weight. And
he has and he will!" That's what he said to all of us. And
then he added, "I can't believe he's dead. He's too good
a fighter to let himself be killed just like that. Find him,
one way or the other." That's what the Major said.

YOUNG ISAAC
You found me first.

ANYA
Before anyone. Before that worm…

YOUNG ISAAC
Wasic…

ANYA
(Faces him. Kisses him. Then holds his face in her hands.)
Before him. Yes. He's coming. I know it. He started

drinking after the Major made his little speech.

YOUNG ISAAC

> Let him come. I'm not worried.

(He tries to stand. Still a bit wobbly. Sits back down, dizzy.)

ANYA

> One more thing, Cricket. You got to know…

YOUNG ISAAC

> More?

(She whispers the news in his ear. Young Isaac kisses her, then looks at her with concern.)

> You're sure…?

(She nods.)

ANYA

> If it gets out, the Major will be forced to ship me back to Russia. I don't want to leave. I want to be here, near you and keep fighting until the war ends, for us.

YOUNG ISAAC

> Yes! You must! For you and me and the child. We must stay together. A family. A new family! Our family. A Bruchka!

(Anya looks questioningly at him.)

> A blessing! Our child.

ANYA

> Yes.

(Pronouncing word carefully.)

> Our Bruchka.

(He hugs her carefully, kissing her on the cheek.)

> I'll try and cover it up so it doesn't show as long as I can. Until I can't hide it any longer. But if I'm sent away, you must come to me, when it's safe, but as soon as you can. I'll be waiting for you with our child…our "bruchka" in Brovary, near Kyev Ostrov. But it must be our secret until then. There's no other way.

(She kisses him.)

> Promise.

YOUNG ISAAC

Are you sure? If you are in any danger…

ANYA

Please. Trust me. If I must leave, you will come to me.
Promise.

YOUNG ISAAC

Promise.
(He takes her hand.)
(Sudden gunshot. A shout offstage.)

WASIC (O.S.)

Get away from him, Anya. Get away from that
lowlife, lying dog of a Jew.
(Wasic appears with a pistol pointed in their direction. He is drunk.)
It's you I want! You, Isaac, and all your filthy
Jewish scum! You're the reason for the war and all our
troubles!

YOUNG ISAAC
(Trying to stand.)

Give me your rifle. Anya! Move away.
(Anya steps away from Isaac, moves to confront Wasic. Hangs on to her
rifle, pointing it at Wasic, who stops.)

WASIC

Not you, Anya. It's him I want. That runt pig. Not you.
Move away.

YOUNG ISAAC
(Tries to shelter Anya, grabbing her rifle. She pulls it away.)

He wants me, not you! Anya…!

ANYA
(To Wasic)

No one is getting what they want! Do you hear me,
Wasic? Not today. No one!
(She walks toward Wasic, her rifle pointed at him, her finger on the trigger.)
(Young Isaac, still reeling from the blow to his head, grabs Anya by the
shoulders and tries to pull her back. She is startled and her rifle goes off.

Lights fade on scene scene.)
(Lights brighten on Old Isaac still sitting on bed, painfully reliving the memory. We hear one more quick shot.)

ISAAC
(He cries out in English and Yiddish.)
No! No! Meyn Got! Anya. Anya!
(He stands. Puts on his cap, then his long coat with some difficulty, looks around, ready to leave.)
(Lights fade)
(In the dark we hear a door creak open and shut.)

SCENE TEN

(Lights up on Anna. Sitting outside of Isaac's room. She is awakened by the noise of the door. Disoriented. She suddenly realized the satchel and care are missing. She stands up abruptly.)
(The scene is in English.)

ANNA
(Shouting.)
> **What have you done with Isaac's belongings? You have no right to take it. Do you hear me!**

(Mercedes runs in, shushing her.)

MERCEDES
> **Miss Brown. Please. It's late. You mustn't…**

ANNA
> **Look! Everything I brought him. Missing. Missing.**

MERCEDES
> **Please, don't shout.**

ANNA
> **I'll shout until I get an answer. Why did you take it?**

MERCEDES
> **Me? I've been upstairs all this time. We're having problems with that lady I told you about. The Duchess with her English castle.**

ANNA
> **Who took them?**

(Mercedes looks around. She sees the door to Isaac's room is open.)

MERCEDES
> **His door. Did you go in? Did you forget to close it?**

ANNA
> **What?**

MERCEDES

His door. Isaac's door is wide open.

(Mercedes looks in.)

Issac! Mr. Hochman.

(Walks out)

He took his coat and hat. He's just wearing pajamas and he wanders off in the middle of winter. The poor man. We'll find him.

ANNA

He took everything.

MERCEDES

I told you I was concerned. Believe me, I want him back safe and sound in our home as much as you.

(She runs out to get Security.)

ANNA

(To Mercedes, who is not listening.)

Home? This is no home for him.

(Lights fade)

SCENE ELEVEN

(Night time. Christmas lights blinking in the distance.
Sound of rushing water and wind. Occasional sound of cars honk-
ing in the distance.)
(Lights up on Isaac, in his worn-out long coat, his Russian mouton
hat with the flaps, leaning on the cane and holding his satchel.)
(He has been walking for over an hour, lost, in so many ways,
until he finds his bench.)
(He sits on his bench by the river. Sound of rushing water. Opens
satchel to take out the map and discovers a wad of money. He
holds the bills in his hand, puzzled, looking at it.)
(Young Man One goes by, sees Isaac with the money and takes off.
Isaac barely notices him.)
(He stuffs the money back into satchel. He is tired, breathless.)
(He closes his eyes.)
(Lights up, blindingly bright.)
(In Isaac's memory, it is suddenly daytime, Young Isaac appears,
playing out the scene that Isaac is remembering and reliving.
Sound of knocking.)

YOUNG ISAAC
(In front of his old house in Rovno.)
(Kcholp, the Polish Fireman, enters. Young Isaac confronts him, holding
the map.)
(They speak in Polish.)

KCHOLP

You? Alive? You have no business coming back here.
The war is over. This is not your house anymore, if that's
what you're thinking. Not your house, not your country.
Not anything!

YOUNG ISAAC

Please, Kcholp. I need to rest. I have a long way to go.
Many kilometers west of here, see. Near Kyev Ostrov.
(Tries to show him location on map.)

KCHOLP

You can go to hell for all I care.

YOUNG ISAAC

I've been told not to go on into Russia. I won't be welcome.

KCHOLP

You're not welcome anywhere. Not there. Not here. Not anywhere.

YOUNG ISAAC

I don't care. I have to try and get back to her, to my Anya and my child. I just need to rest. You owe me just a moment. Some food. Some rest.

KCHOLP

I owe you nothing. I gave you and your father a chance to give me a measly painting of wildflowers and that gilded mirror. What good was a mirror to you and your people? You don't need a mirror. Why would you want to look at yourself? I don't want to look at you. Get off my property.
(Kcholp reaches for a cane resting near his door and threatens him with it.)
Or I'll make you.

YOUNG ISAAC

That cane. I know it....It was my Zayda's.

KCHOLP

Get off my steps.

YOUNG ISAAC

I put it by the door before we left. His cane with the brass handle and silver tip.

KCHOLP

Before I call the authorities, start moving!

YOUNG ISAAC

You have no right...

KCHOLP
(Laughs shrilly)

Rights? You're the one without any rights. You don't
even have the right to live but you go on breaking the
law by breathing.

YOUNG ISAAC

Do you know how many people died so you could have
that cane and this house?

KCHOLP

Why did they let you live? You should be dead. They
should have killed you and dumped you in that ditch
with the rest of your filthy family. Like a drowned rat!
That's all you are, a naked disgusting, rat-faced Jew who
doesn't know he's dead! Climb back into that ditch with
the others.
(He hits Young Isaac with the cane. Young Isaac doesn't move. He doesn't
feel the external pain.)
You're dead! Dead!
(Strikes him again. Old Isaac cringes with the memory of the blows.
Young Isaac takes the blows without reacting.)
You don't know it. But that's what you are. Dead!
(Lights darken. Image of Kcholp and Young Isaac face. It is night time
again. Isaac still sits on the bench, shaking from the memory. He looks
around. Still lost.)
(Lights dim on him.)
(Lights up on Anna who appears on the other side of the stage. She is
dressed in heavy coat, wearing Wool hat and gloves. She holds a photo of
Isaac in her gloved hand. She will move along the edge of the stage as if
showing the photo to pedestrians going by.)
(She speaks in English.)

ANNA

His name is Isaac. He sometimes calls himself Sergei.
Here. Here's his photo. If you see him, call 911. Please.
Just look. You can at least look. He's not dangerous, I
swear. He just wants to get home. Where are you running? Just glance at his face. That's all I ask. He answers
to the name of Isaac or Sergei. Call 911 if you…What
did you say? It's not a joke. He's lost. Have some care.
Some mercy. I'm not asking for money. Fine. Ignore me.
Merry Christmas. Peace be with you.

(Lights fade on Anna.)

(Lights up on Isaac on his bench. Sound of a plane overhead triggers Isaac's memo memory. Lights brighten into daytime.)

(Lights up on Alyosha, the grizzled, one-eyed veteran. It is right after the war and Alyosha is now trying to look like a civilian wearing a shabby, oversized suit jacket, a collarless shirt with a tie. Young Isaac appears again, playing out the scene. Old Isaac, still sitting on the bench, relives it all over again.)

(Young Isaac approaches Alyosha from behind. Taps him on the back, holding the map.)

(They speak in Russian.)

YOUNG ISAAC

(Pointing to location on map.)

Sir, I am looking for this. What is the name of your village? Am I near Kyev Ostrov? I've been traveling for days.

(Alyosha turns around.)

ALYOSHA

(Turn around, annoyed at first. Then looks intently at Isaac.)

Sergei? It can't be!

(Alyosha wears a suit and tie.)

YOUNG ISAAC

Alyosha! Look at you! A gentleman!

ALYOSHA

(Hugs him.)

I don't believe it. Sergei!

YOUNG ISAAC

The war is over, Alyosha. I'm Isaac again.

ALYOSHA

Of course. Yes. Dear Isaac. But why…?

YOUNG ISAAC

It's my name.

ALYOSHA

No. Why have you come back?

YOUNG ISAAC
For Anya…

ALYOSHA
No.

YOUNG ISAAC
And my child. I have never seen my child. I don't even know if I have a son or a daughter. But Anya is waiting. She should be close. Here, on the map, Brovary, near Kyev Ostrov.
(Points to map.)
See. I'm sure I am no more than 15 kilometers away from her.

ALYOSHA
But…No.

YOUNG ISAAC
Yes! Look. At the map. How close…

ALYOSHA
Isaac, she's gone.

YOUNG ISAAC
From the Brigade, yes; from the forest, from the war. Back to Kyev. I know. After Wasic wounded her, the Major flew her back to Russia so she can get the proper medical attention.

ALYOSHA
Still, Sergei…Isaac…you must know…

YOUNG ISAAC
I know Anya is waiting. My child is waiting. They are the only family I have left. And they are waiting to greet me and embrace me. We will all be together soon.

ALYOSHA
You have to listen to me.

YOUNG ISAAC

We worked it all out, Anya and me. I know I'm near.

ALYOSHA

My God, Isaac. Don't go. There's no reason…It's too dangerous. Believe me, it's a bad time for you, for your people. Go back.

YOUNG ISAAC

Thank you for all your concern, Alyosha. But there is all the reason in the world for me to go on. I'll get through. Anya is waiting. My child is waiting.

ALYOSHA

They're not waiting. No one is waiting.
(Lights darken)
The Major didn't get word about Anya for months.
It was too late by then. We had all scattered to the wind.
It was too late to get word to you, to tell you.

YOUNG ISAAC

Tell me what? What are you saying?

ALYOSHA

Anya died in a hospital near Kyev from Wasic's gunshot.
She's gone. The baby died. The Major was never told
whether it was a boy or a girl. I'm sorry, so sorry.
(Lights fade on Alyosha and Young Isaac.)
(Night time. Isaac sits on the bench. He is sobbing, remembering the encounter with Alyosha.)

ISAAC (IN YIDDISH)

Anya. Meyn Anya…Meyn Kind.
(Sound of rushing water increases.)
(Light up on two Young Men.)
(They speak in English.)

FIRST YOUNG MAN

What did I tell ya? Check out the bag he's carrying.
Plenty green. I'm tellin' ya he got a pile of greens in that piece of shit bag.

SECOND YOUNG MAN
> You didn't tell me he's just an old man. Let's forget it.

FIRST YOUNG MAN
> Are you shitting me?
(Isaac turns and sees them. He stands with the help of his cane.)
> What is this?

FIRST YOUNG MAN
(First Young Man kicks the cane out of Isaac's hand. Isaac collapses on ground. First Young Man puts his foot on Isaac's back. Isaac still clutches his satchel.)
(To Isaac.)
> Gotchya! You ain't going nowhere.
(To Second Young Man.)
> Don't just stand there like a fucking log. Grab his bag. What's with you? Lose your fucking nerve?

SECOND YOUNG MAN
> I don't know. This just don't feel right.

FIRST YOUNG MAN
(First Young Man grabs satchel out of Isaac's hand and spills out Josef's money and some of Isaac's handwritten yellow pages.)
(To Second Young Man.)
> Told ya! Nice fucking haul. I got this old fart. Take it! Now! Get the fucking lead out, now!

SECOND YOUNG MAN
(He picks up money.)
> We're done. Right? Let's get the hell outta here.

ISAAC
> Beasts! Nazi Khius!

FIRST YOUNG MAN
> What's he screaming Nazi shit? Look at him. A fuckin' roach...

SECOND YOUNG MAN
> We got the money. Leave him the fuck alone!

FIRST YOUNG MAN

I could squash him just like that.
(Lifts his foot over Isaac's head.)
(Second Young Man pushes him off Isaac. Young Man One pushes him
back angrily and puts foot on Isaac's back.)
Don't ever push me! What's got into you?

SECOND YOUNG MAN

**Just an old man. Old as hell. Not worth spit.
Let's just get outta here. Now!**

FIRST YOUNG MAN

Don't tell me what to do. Grow a pair!

SECOND YOUNG MAN

Fuck you!
(Anna appears.)

ANNA

**Isaac! What are you doing to him? Let him go! Take
whatever you want. Just let him go!**

FIRST YOUNG MAN

Look at her. Old man, you have good taste.

ANNA

**That's enough. I won't call the police if you just take off
now. Don't hurt him. Please.**

FIRST YOUNG MAN

Did you hear that? She's begging us.
(He takes his foot off Isaac and moves towards Anna.)
Whoa. We got something going here. Right?
(He grabs Anna.)
(She tries to pull away but he puts his hand over her mouth.)
Don't fight, bitch.
(To Second Young Man.)
**Forget the old fart. He ain't goin' nowhere.
We got easy pickins here.**
(He screams at Second Young Man who stands frozen.)

What's got into you?

SECOND YOUNG MAN
Let her go. She's got nothing…

FIRST YOUNG MAN
(Anna struggles.)
Now. Now. Don't make me hurt you bad.
(To Second Young Man.)
Grab her feet. Hear me? Grab her…

SECOND YOUNG MAN
(Throws down money.)
I want no part of this. Screw you! I'm done!
(He runs off.)

FIRST YOUNG MAN
(To Second Young Man.)
Where ya goin'? We ain't done, you chicken shit!
(He lets go of Anna to reach for money and she kicks him.)

ANNA
Filthy bastard!
(He grabs her with one arm and pulls out a knife. He starts to drag her into the shadows.)

FIRST YOUNG MAN
I'll shut you up now real good!
(Isaac sees what is happening, struggles to his feet, grabbing his cane.)

ISAAC
(He shouts in German.)
You want to see this cane. Here! Here!
(He comes at him with his cane, striking him across the head.)

FIRST YOUNG MAN
(Lets go of Anna.)

ISAAC
Run, Anya! It's me he wants.
(Isaac strikes the young man with cane again.)

ANNA

Help! Someone! Police! Someone!
(She runs off.)

ISAAC

Nazi beast!
(Isaac raises his cane to strike him again.)

FIRST YOUNG MAN

Fuckin' old…I'll Nazi you!
(He stabs Isaac, but Isaac brings his cane down on the young man's hand
and knocks the knife out of his grip, then collapses to the ground.)
(Sound of sirens in the distance.)

Shit!
(He picks up his knife and rushes off.)
(Sirens diminish.)
(Isaac, in pain, lifts himself and sits on the bench.)
(Sound of rushing water.)
(Lights blindingly bright again, enveloping the stage. Anya appears. Isaac
sees her. She speaks in Russian.)

ANYA

**…by the eddies where the rivers cross…
I'm waiting…Come soon. Soon…**
(Sound of rushing water increases, deafening. Then lights fade, silence.)
(Sound of phone ringing.)

SCENE TWELVE

(Phone continues to ring. Lights up on Josef in Isaac's apartment.
Isaac's pages are scattered over the kitchen table Next to the satchel.)
(Josef picks up the phone.)
(He speaks in English.)

JOSEF

> Yes. I'm here, Anna. How is he?…Now, don't cry. He's a
> tough old bird….Yes. Yes, I'll bring his satchel.
> Promise…I'll get everything together for him…
> Yes, I know. I know…Love you, too.

(He hangs up. Gathers Isaac's pages scattered on the table, but starts to
read Isaac's account. Projection of yellow pages turning.)
(Lights fade to low as Josef reads.)
(Cross-fade on Old Isaac speaking words from pages.)
(Old Isaac speaks in Yiddish.)

ISAAC

> I write so I remember. I must not forget. I'm afraid I
> will…No! I will not forget. Sol, Mameh, Tateh, Anya.
> Oh Anya! My pure and holy one. My love. I must not
> forget YOU. You must not be forgotten. Never! I must
> remember everything. Everyone. So I write…I write…I
> write…

(Lights dim to out on Old Isaac, Josef and pages.)

SCENE THIRTEEN

(Lights up on Anna sitting at Isaac's kitchen table. She is wearing a black dress. Isaac's satchel sits on the table along with his cane and Russian hat. His winter overcoat is draped over the chair.)
(Josef enters. He is wearing a black suit under a dark overcoat.)
(They speak in English.)

JOSEF

We're ready.

ANNA

Give me a moment.

JOSEF

Anna, I have our limo and Isaac's hearse waiting outside.

ANNA

Isaac is done wandering. Let him rest.

JOSEF

What about all that?
(Motions to the objects on the table.)
What do you want me to do with it?

ANNA
(Thinks for a moment.)
He'll need his cane and his hat. Both of them go with him.

JOSEF

Whatever you say. Fine.

ANNA

And his long coat.

JOSEF

Are you sure?

ANNA

He will be cold.

JOSEF

Anna, I will do anything for him that you ask. He saved your life. But does it really matter if we leave some of his stuff behind?

ANNA

There is enough room I'm sure.

JOSEF

I'm sure there is.

ANNA

You know I signed papers for Louis. For the new apartment.

JOSEF

I know. I'm relieved. Too many memories in this place. Important to start fresh.

ANNA

I'm keeping all of Sergei's papers.

JOSEF

Whose?

ANNA

Isaac's, I mean. Some blew away when those punks…I'll keep what's left in his satchel. It's only right. I'll take them with me to my…new home. It's too easy to forget.

JOSEF

I understand.

ANNA

He will be next to his Sarah?

JOSEF

All arranged. Louis contacted his own Rabbi. They'll

meet us there.

ANNA

There was no one to call. He left no numbers, no names.

JOSEF

We'll be there. He won't be alone.

ANNA

I love you, Josef. He would be pleased to know how much you have done for him.

(Josef walks to the table, kisses Anna on the cheek.)

JOSEF

I read some of his papers, you know.

ANNA

When?

JOSEF

When you were sitting in the hospital just before he died. You asked me to go to his apartment and bring that satchel to you.

ANNA

Yes.

JOSEF

I saw his papers spread out on the table like they were waiting to be read. I don't know what possessed me but I sat down and started to read.

ANNA

Really?

JOSEF

Read about the death of his brother and his family and all the horror of their last days.

ANNA

So much suffering.

JOSEF

> And when I finished, I just sat there. Didn't move. I suddenly felt cold. Colder than I have ever felt before.

ANNA

> I know that feeling. When Mother died and when Isaac died, I felt that cold. Like a fist of ice in my chest. I was too weak to cry or move.

JOSEF

> I realized I was deathly afraid I'd find Father's name, his real German name, in those pages of Isaac's.

ANNA

> He's not there.

JOSEF

> No. He's not, but he could have been. That's what got to me. I kept wondering if he could have been one of those…Nazi monsters. The ones I saw in movies and read about, the ones who killed millions and millions of Isaacs. Maybe…maybe he was part of the horror. Isaac's horror. The war's horror. And, god forgive me, just for a moment, reading Isaac's words, I wanted him dead. I wanted my own father dead! I didn't feel a bit of sorrow or grief or guilt. Only that awful cold. But it's not right to feel that way. It's just not right!

ANNA

> It's time to bury Father as well.

JOSEF

> Yes.

ANNA

> Maybe he was just that. Our father. That's all we know for sure.

JOSEF

> Yes.

ANNA
(She stands and embraces him.)
Yes. Leave it at that.

JOSEF
You're right.
(Steps back and looks at her.)
Anna, look at you. I don't think I've seen you in a dress for years.

ANNA
(Smiles)
It was mother's. Her basic black. She was always prepared for mourning.

JOSEF
Wait. Louis reminded me.
(Takes out a torn black ribbon and kippah from his coat pocket. He pins the torn black black ribbon on his lapel and puts the yarmulke on his head.)
There.
(Anna puts on a lacy scarf over her head.)
We're ready for Isaac. Oh yes. This.
(Reaches into the inside pocket of his suit and pulls out two cards with English and Hebrew writing on it.)
Here.
(Gives one card to Anna.)
Louis said we read this at the grave site.
(Stumbling, mispronouncing.)
Yit-ga-dull Ve-yeee- ga-dish shee-my ra-beee…

ANNA
You can read it in English. Isaac won't mind.

JOSEF
That I can do.
(Reads)
"Glorified and Sanctified be God's great name throughout the World which He has created according to his will." I got it. Now I'm ready.

(Starts to gather up the cane, hat, and long coat. Reaches for the satchel, but Anna stops him from taking the satchel.)

ANNA

You got your arms full. I want to carry something.

JOSEF

No problem.

ANNA

I'll keep the satchel in the limo and bring it home with me.

(He starts to exit. Anna holds back.)

JOSEF

We're going? Right?

ANNA

I'll be down in a minute. Have to finish up. I need one last moment alone.

JOSEF

I understand.

(He kisses Anna.)

I really understand.

(He exits.)

(Anna sits at the table. Starts putting Isaac's pages tenderly into the satchel. She pauses.)

(Young Isaac appears behind her. She senses a presence. She speaks to it without turning.)

Isaac?

(Young Isaac speaks in Russian.)

YOUNG ISAAC

Anya. Anya, it's me. Your Sergei, your Isaac.

(Anna does not hear the words and is not frightened, but she does not turn around. She smiles, feeling he is near her.)

I knew you would be here. Waiting.

(Sound of rushing water. He kisses the tips of his fingers then reaches out to almost stroke Anna gently on the side of her cheek, but doesn't touch her. Anna brush brushes her hand across her cheek as if she has felt

something.)
(Lights up on Old Isaac in overcoat and mouton cap, leaning on his cane.)
(Young Isaac whispers to Anna in Russian.)

I'm home, Anya.

ISAAC
(Isaac whispers to Anna in Yiddish.)

I'm home.

(Lights dim on Young and Old Isaac. They stand in place, watching Anna.)
(Anna turns, but does not see them.)
(She touches her cheek again, then finishes placing Isaac's pages into the satchel.)
(She puts on her overcoat and picks up the satchel. Then takes the Kaddish card on the table without looking at it and puts it in the satchel. Then she lifts the satchel, clutching it close to her body with both arms, embracing it and begins to recite recite the Kaddish perfectly, quietly, poignantly.)
(Lights fade slowly on all of them as she recites.)

ANNA

Yitgadal V'yitkadash sh'mei raba b'alma di-'v'ra chirutei, v'yamlich malchutei…

(They all freeze in place.)
(Silence.)
(Projection of Isaac's handwritten pages. Slow dissolve of one page after the other in the silence.)
(Fade to black.)

END OF PLAY

FIVE STORIES OF ISAAC'S LIFE,
HIS FAMILY, FRIENDS AND HOME
PRIOR TO WORLD WAR II

CHAPTER ONE

THE MEDIEVAL GATES

They breeched the crumbled walls of the Koscioweski Castle. Isaac led the way. Even though he was the shortest and thinnest, he was the most agile and nimble. He scampered over the fortress wall surrounding the thirteenth century palace of this Polish prince. Isaac's school friends followed him, frantically looking about for some policemen or farmer to spot their trespassing and seize them like common bandits.

Through a large chink in the wall of rubble, the boys scrambled towards the central gate, up a twisted stone stairway, stone and dirt crumbling under their heels as they ascended.

Hagar, Isaac's very best friend, loved to read about adventure just the same as Isaac. Hagar was tall, lanky with straight black hair and projecting bushy eyebrows that gave his face the look of mystery and menace. But he was no more menacing than a field- mouse and no more mysterious than a lamb. The other friend, Morris, was broader, stronger looking than both, but he had a nervous twitter of a voice that stammered and stuttered in front of teachers, bullies, sharpies and any girl. It was only with Isaac and Hagar that Morris talked straight and confidently, except now.

As they entered the inner precincts of the castle through a broken iron gate, Morris stopped suddenly and shouted, as much as could shout in his squeaky, birdlike twitter. "Isaac, Di…Di…Did you hear th…that?" The boys stopped. In the warm, woozy Polish afternoon, you could hear the whirr and click of crickets and locusts from the white birch groves, and the distant yelping of dogs from the nearby yard of Karl Lodz, the town dog-catcher. Maybe a wagon was heard as well, rumbling and creaking down a dirt road. The boys held their breath. That was all. Nothing else. Everything was normal. Isaac turned to Morris, his lean, thoughtful face broke out in a comforting smile.

"Morry. Morry. We're all alone here. Perfectly safe. Trust me."

With that, Isaac plunged on. Among the few friends who knew him well, Isaac was a steady, reliable friend. For a fourteen-year-old, he was unusually inquisitive and studious. But there was the private romantic side as well, nourished by his family's library, the largest in town, full of forbidden books by continental authors, like Maupassant and Balzac along with a complete collection of Tarzan books. He would lend his prized books out to his two friends only, knowing they too hungered for the fantasies and escapes.

At night, Isaac could close his eyes after hours of reading and transform the dusty, graven-strewn landscape of his town of Rovne, into a dark jungle of vines, gorillas, and stealthy predators. Even this ruined Polish castle, once a grand and powerful residence, could be changed into a secret jungle stronghold full of monstrous sultans and savage emperors.

Isaac had no doubt that any minute they would confront some hooded assailant from behind a lichen-covered boulder or grapple with a giant python curling down from an overhanging beam.

Morris and Hagar followed him, excited by his sense of exploration, fleeing the less inviting world of their Polish schoolmates. Like Isaac, they were just too insecure to keep up with the more athletic, fashionable and worldly. They were no match for the sons and daughters of actors, politicians and merchants. Like Isaac, they were too slight or awkward to fool the girls who were able to sniff out their congenital shyness and giggle at their gawky ways.

So there they were, a band of three intrepid Polish schoolboys, seeking out the mysterious interior of a medieval palace that they had always read about in their history books. To Hagar and Morris, it was just a game, but Isaac needed to know about everything. Whether it was current politics or a new math formula or the most outlandish fantasy, he could not help but explore it to its limits.

Most of the castle had been destroyed by fires and storm. Roofs had collapsed, walls had tumbled, but there was still the central hall with its hidden metal door leading to subterranean passageways. The boys had never come this far before. But Isaac goaded them on, intent on unlocking the secrets of the castle's underground vaults.

Pushing away a tilting oak door, he entered the great hall. Sunlight poured down between charred and rotting timbers. Without looking back once to check for his friends, he ran toward the metal door with the great iron ring. Rocks and timber snarled at him each time he tugged harder and harder. Hagar caught up with him to help and they both pulled, while Morris held back, staring up at the shattered roof, waiting for everything to collapse upon them. A bit of dust fell from the overhanging beams and a pebble struck Morris on the shoulder. He screamed. "It will fall on top of us, everything. And we'll never get out."

Hagar kidded him. "Watch it, Murry, the sky is falling. The sky is falling!" It was harmless mockery but Morris was hurt. Isaac saw Morris's face turn sour.

"Don't worry. Nothing will happen, Murry. Believe me."

Then Hagar and Isaac continued to pull at the door. They made a funny picture in the filtering light. Hagar was at least a foot taller than Isaac. His dark brooding face contrasted sharply with Isaac's pale lean look. Though monastically thin, Isaac still had a luminous sparkle to his eyes and a radiant vitality to his smile. Given his personality and character, Isaac should have been a foot taller and fifty pounds heavier. His abundant spirit betrayed a seemingly ascetic physique that he had inherited from his father. Along with the body, he had inherited a premature widow's peak that gave him a decidedly intellectual look.

With a final effort, Hagar and Isaac opened the metal door wide enough to squeeze through. Morris was terrified at the thought of going any further, but Isaac had no hesitation. He quickly lit a lantern he had hooked on his belt and began to descend into the underground corridors. Hagar followed, his tall form stopped beneath the low roof.

"I'll st…st…stand guard!" Morris announced.

Isaac nodded and continued into the darkness. Groping along the walls, they inched forward, with the lantern light surrounding them in a small sphere of illumination. It grew darker and darker, almost as if with each step forward, they moved backward into another century. The air grew closer, danker, thick as fog about them. Isaac could almost touch and smell history about him…eighteenth century, seventeenth century, back toward the dark ages, they descended…fourteenth century, thirteenth. Then, Isaac saw the doors. In the light, they looked like wooden shields with barred crests. But closer up, Isaac recognized what they were. Prison cells for the enemies of Prince Koscioweski. He held the lantern beside the barred windows and peered inside. But the lantern could not penetrate the almost smoky blackness. So, Isaac pulled at the door. Hagar hung close to him, totally dependent now on Isaac's courage. With the prison door opened wide enough, Isaac shoved through. At the entrance, he held the lantern up once again and this time he could see to the very ends of the stony walls.

In one corner, he made out a large wooden wheel encircled with iron spikes and fitted with rings and metal hoops. Shreds of leather straps, now half rotted away, were visible. Next to it a cylindrical cage with a long manacle and chain hanging from its peaked top. And then, as Isaac turned the lantern toward the far left corner, he saw what seemed like a grey, stony skull…the lantern giving the hollow apertures of the face a life-like glint. For a moment, Isaac thought he saw it smile and in the wavering shadows of the hand-held lantern, he swore it moved—just an inch toward him. Even for Isaac, this was too much adventure, and abruptly and violently, he backed out, knocking Hagar to the dirt floor. He didn't utter a sound, but started to run, and Hagar, picking up the scent of terror, screamed after him. They bumped and groped down the corridor, not even worrying about the lantern's direction. Instinct carried them up the stairs, toward the metal door and the twentieth century. Isaac heard Hagar screaming and panting, but he still remained quiet while fleeing in panic. When Morris heard Hagar scream, he started to shake. He backed off, afraid to see what would emerge from the portal; suddenly Hagar burst through. He kept running right through the rubble, over the wall into the pasture, and down the main road to home. Morris, sensing danger, followed Hagar, leaping over the stones until he found his path and sprinted home.

Only Isaac was left in the main hall when he finally emerged from the underground passages. He stopped, looked around, felt an urge to run, but in the sunlight, it seemed unnecessary. He blew out his lantern, hooked it to his belt, thought of his good friends speeding away from the unknown, and he started to laugh. This was better than any story. This was history. This was truth. The thought of the torturous machines and battered skulls below made him shiver. But then he thought of his warm kitchen, his mother's stew cooking since morning, and the mahogany radio playing music and news in the evening through the open window, so all the neighbors could listen. And he felt safe and secure once again and started to hike home through the modern landscape of his beloved Rovne. Looking one more time at the castle behind him, he saw it for the first time in all its medieval grotesqueness and realized how wonderful it was to be alive in this year of 1939.

CHAPTER TWO

THE MILLSTONES GRIND

Isaac always took the short cut home, through the woods. Unlike Hagar and Morris, he avoided the worn ruts and gashes of the well-traveled roads and blazed his own trails through the white birch forest of the Sussenkess, skirting as quietly and carefully as possible the ram-shackled yellow sheds of Goetz, the dogcatcher. He loved the dense woods the most and the blind plunge through the brush and branches. Just like his father, Isaac felt at home in the solitude of nature.

About a mile from the white birch grove, he began smelling his house. To anyone else, the smell was harsh and sour. His family's business, started by his grandfather, was the curing of skins and hides, and the stretching of the skins gave off a dense acrid odor that literally drove the neighbors away. But Isaac grew up in the center of the thriving business. It was the fragrance of family to him. And even at a mile away, he could sniff out his mother's thick, molten stew simmering in the kettle by the window.

At a small rise just above the family's factory and home, he could see all of Rovne stretching out in the flat, dusty plains between the Polessi marshes and the Sussenkess birch groves behind him. The heavily populated Jewish section of town was dominated by the towering stained glass windows of the Gochev Synagogue. Even from this far distance, Isaac could make out the glowing image of the twin trees of Paradise depicted in the great stained glass windows—the Tree of Life and the Tree of Knowledge. Just beyond the proud edifice of the synagogue was the open, tent-draped stalls of the market-place, always crowded with shoppers full of exotic goods from far flung reaches of a world Isaac had never seen.

Closer to home, Isaac could now taste the stew in the air. No curing hides could deflect his appetite. He rushed on, past his family's factory, past the workers near the curing barn, tending the gray hanging rows of drying skins that looked like giant bat wings from a distance. Near the barn, he stopped for a moment to look for his father or grandfather. They would often stay late in the mid-week of summer to help. But he could not find them. There were only the four horses at the center of the activity, yoked to a great metal axle, moving slowly in a circle hour after hour, goaded on by the other workers, and there, turning as surely as the seasons turn was the center of the family's fortune: two giant circular millstones, as large across the diameter as the towering Hagar, grinding and creaking in their revolutions day and night. Between the stones, the skins and hides were placed to be pressed and stretched slowly and inexorably. A worker would step in every half hour between the leather rings of the horses lashed to the millstone to wet the hides with chemicals and water. Round and round, grinding and stretching, the millstones never stopped now that the demand for his family's goods was so great. Day and night, Isaac could hear the rumble of the axis and almost pretend to hear the taut skins stretching achingly slow under the pressure. When he was younger and even more fanciful, Isaac imagined this place of millstones as the very center of earth and the sound, the very noise of the globe turning on its gears. He knew better now, but the noise of the grinding was still inescapable, a reliable clock ticking away with certainty and good fortune.

Isaac waved to some of the workers, who grinned back, and then he started toward his homestead. By the end of one road leading to his house, stood a brightly colored house with scrollwork and scalloped casements, a kind of gingerbread house in wood with curves and wiggles. It had once belonged to a Polish carpenter who, years before, retreated from the smell of the hides and sold the house to Isaac's grandfather.

This had been the fate of most of the homes surrounding the plant. But this particular house was Isaac's favorite. His grandfather had promised it to him when he reached maturity and took on a wife and family. It was perfect. Besides, it was the house his mother had always rented to actors and singers who traveled in the warm weather, trouping on the road between Warsaw and Brest. It was rented once again this summer to a Yiddish theatrical group, and the house had been full of grand speeches and lilting music for a week.

Isaac's mother, Hindle, a beautiful, shapely woman with fine bones and an elegant face, would often take Isaac with her in the early evening for a stroll by the house. He never understood why at first, but as they reached the walk leading to the front door, his mother would stop, listen for a moment to the constant theatrics inside—high pitched singing of some new theater song—and watch shadows behind the curtains of high-bosomed, tight-waisted ladies gesticulating wildly in the air, intoning lofty speeches with earthy Yiddish inflections. Then, Isaac's mother would start to hum and, perhaps, sing quietly a few lines of her favorite Austrian or Swiss folk song. She could sing in German or French or Yiddish and would often mix the languages in one song to impress the theatrical audience busy within the rented house. That was the intention after all, Isaac figured out as he got older. His mother wanted this free-spirited, cosmopolitan troupe to hear her singing and acknowledge her talent. He was sure she would never run away with them because she always left the house with something cooking on the stove, but he was also sure that she needed such an audience to applaud her melodic voice and cultured tones. No one could be any more beautiful and any more distinguished than his mother, but her destiny as a performer had led to this great family house and to the nightly routine of lullabies she would sing to her children at bedtime. Besides, some of Isaac's more worldly companions would whisper stories about these actors that would make a sodomite blush.

With the stew thick and pungent in his mouth now, Isaac could not linger too long in front of this theatrical house. But he did so want to catch, just once, a glimpse between the curtain of some forbidden or wanton practice. He didn't quite know what to look for, but it had to do with the flesh and bosoms and he was sure these actors were adept at it. Besides, just listening gave him a special tingle. They spoke differently than anyone else, no matter what the language, and they gestured in the shadows behind the curtain like princes and princesses, emperors and queens. Nothing was common or mundane. They carried themselves with such confidence, it took Isaac's breath away. Finally, the forbidden urges that led him to peer at the actors gave way to hunger and soon he was running to his house.

He arrived late. There everyone was…his mother, Hindle, elegant and smiling even in her apron, his older brother, the doctor, with his wife, looking prosperous and kindly as he always did, his grandfather sitting in the high-backed chair of the dining room, holding on to an ebony cane with the silver handle that he loved so much, and carried with him to the side of his bed. His grandfather knocked the cane gently against the floor and announced in gravel-pitched tones, "So, our boy, Izzela, decided to eat with us tonight. How good of you, my boy."

The radio was cackling and whining away through the kitchen window, talking about some distant European conference with a seriousness that always scared Isaac. He loved to hear news, but liked the idea of events being far away, beyond the big rivers and the Carpathians. Tonight, he could not hear the words distinctly, but sensed the reporter's tones as being more serious than ever. Though, soon the rush of dinner distracted him.

He walked in the warm, joyous vestibule, took his boots off, laid his lantern down by the great gilded mirror that dominated the foyer, kissed the silver mezuzah by the door-jamb and went inside.

No matter how many entrances he made, Isaac was always proud of the look of his home, with its elegant mirrors and paintings everywhere.

He washed his hands quickly and came to the large table just outside the kitchen. It was the main room of the house where everything was done—eating, celebrating, reading, arguing. Now it was dinner and the table was full of breads and baskets of fruit. And of course at the center, a great porcelain casserole of his mother's beef stew. Only his father, Lazar, was missing. Sill on a business trip to Brest, he supposed.

Grandfather stood up, leaning on his cane dramatically, lifted the bread, said the prayer, and cut it with a flourish. He was a short man, with a strong, tight jaw and thin face, but he had been strong as an ox until this year. In fact, until this year, he had used the cane simply as an accessory. A rare indulgence in personal vanity that made him look taller and grander and even more authoritative. But now he needed the cane, and even with it, he traveled about the lands and business that he had created with less and less frequency. All last week he stayed in bed, coughing and sleeping. But, tonight he seemed himself again and commanded everyone's attention.

Only Isaac's father was missing, and for Isaac that made him just a bit lonely, in spite of all the loving family about. It was not complete, nothing was truly "family" without his father.

They began to eat. Isaac, as usual, was the noisiest and most frantic of all, gulping into a second helping before anyone, and his mother leaning over his shoulder with a ladle ready to give him more but whispering, "Don't rush. There's plenty of time to eat the whole cow." She would almost dance about the table, humming and serving.

Isaac's brother, the most beloved doctor in Rovne, would always have great stories to tell of the farmers and peasants who would come to him free of charge and leave him goats and cheese and apples for payment. He never came to the house without a wagon full of some medical harvest. His wife, a quiet woman from the town, ate almost sheepishly, like she was some distant relative allowed the privilege of joining the grand family from time to time. It was hard to warm up to her, but as for his brother, Isaac adored him and listened to everything he said. In fact, Isaac would often stay for hours in his brother's library just above the clinic in town; he'd read research books and textbooks, and listen at the same time to his brother's diagnosis and prescription. Isaac could talk like a doctor with his friends, impressing them with what seemed to be an intimate knowledge of the most arcane medical lore.

At one point, in the lull between courses, the radio was turned up by his mother in the kitchen. Isaac thought he heard something about armies and troops, but then Grandfather banged his cane and demanded the radio be shut down. It was.

Near dessert, with the ornate and burnished samovar carefully heated up by his mother so tea could be served, the bump and clank of a wagon was heard outside. A voice shouted from the outside. "Doesn't anyone wait for me anymore?"

Isaac ran from the table and threw open the door. There was Lazar, his father, atop the crooked wagon that had traveled thousands of miles already. In the twilight, his father looked like some ghostly apparition, with his pale face and bald head. But as soon as he saw Isaac, he broke out in a toothy smile and it was like sunrise and a break in the clouds. Isaac jumped on the wagon and they both hugged.

"You wouldn't believe what happened today, son. Such events. Not even Jonah had such bad luck."

Then his father laughed, and always loudest before the story was told, to savor it once more privately to himself.

"Don't keep the stories to yourself and your boy. Come inside, Lazar, why don't you!"

The grandfather ordered, banging once again gently on the floor with his cane. With that, Isaac was lifted up in the air by if father's sturdy arms and lowered to the ground. Then his father jumped down beside him, hugged him close and whispered in his ear, "Soon Izzy, we will picnic in the woods again. Just you and me, special."

With the giant millstones grinding and rumbling away behind him like the endless clock of earth, Isaac felt immortal and invincible. Here between father and house, wagon and family, he was at the center of everything that mattered in the universe; and it would always be this way, just as the millstones would always grind day and night.

CHAPTER THREE

THE LITTLE COUNTESS

The Road was absolutely medieval. There were no cobblestones, no flagstones, no paving at all; just gaping ditches, bottomless ruts, pools of mud, and stones, everywhere stones, forcing the wagon to buck and jolt, sway and leap. Hindle's velvet brocade jacket and lacy blouse were spattered with flecks of mud. Her hairdo, so carefully arranged and pinned, had come undone with strands and tresses whipping wildly about her face each time the wagon bounced.

When Hindle had arrived an hour before at the Rovne railroad station, she was still the vision of a radiant newly-wed, freshly arrived in Eastern Poland from the great city of Zurich, elegant in her Swiss jacket, long draped skirt and flowery hat with silk trim. Next to her stood Lazar, her proud husband of six months, returning home with his beautiful bride from the west.

But, when Hindle stepped onto the crude wooden planks of the station's platform and saw the bare, tin-roofed shed that served as the station master's office, ticket counter, waiting room and cafe, she knew something was wrong. This was nothing like the railroad station in her beloved Zurich with its pavilioned ceiling of crystal and glass supported by steel girders vaulting from floor to roof like the buttresses of a grand cathedral. Rovne's station was a cow shed compared to Zurich's. Lazar saw his wife's look of dismay and disappointment and shrugged his shoulders as he put his arm around her.

He said, "My little countess is disappointed?"

Loving his affectionate use of an imaginary title, Hindle could not bring herself to criticize or complain so quickly about Lazar's birthplace. After all, she had only arrived and, besides, she loved him too much to regret anything he wanted to share with her.

"Oh, no, darling. I'm just so shocked by the air. It smells wonderful. I thought only mountain air could smell this sweet and fresh."

That's all Lazar needed. He clapped his hands and the family draft wagon appeared. On the buckboard, driving the one old horse, was a Ukrainian worker from the tanning plant, with dark, creased skin and cracked, bleached lips. Lazar's father had sent the wagon and driver to pick up his son and his new bride.

Hindle tried to ignore the sight of the wagon. Obviously, this was not Zurich or Vienna. There was no Bahnhofstrasse or Schönbrunn Palace in sight, no sleek carriages, gilded coaches or romantic cabriolets with uniformed lackeys and drivers, or elegant teams of horses festooned with feathers and silver buckles. No, this was Rovne, where a wagon more suitable for transporting radishes and turnips would serve equally as well as a conveyance for "ladies" and "little countesses."

She nodded graciously to the driver who seemed stumped for a moment on how to react. Then, abruptly, he lifted his leather cap high in the air, breaking out in a broad, jagged smile, more of a cheer than a greeting.

At least, Hindle thought, *at least he tipped his cap. All is not lost out here in the wilds.*

With a flourish, Lazar gathered up his new wife in his arms and settled her gently on the wagon seat and they were off, to travel even further east toward Lazar's family home.

With each passing kilometer, the trip grew rougher, and more barbaric along with Hindle's appearance, until she felt as muddy and disheveled as the road. At one point, the wagon struck a bolder, bucked like a horse and tossed Hindle into the air like a sack of feathers. Lazar grabbed her waist, shouting with exhilaration, "hang on Hindella! Don't you dare try to fly away from me now!"

To Lazar, everything was an adventure. He could turn the most mundane event into a romantic interlude, and some banal chore in to a heroic feat, always plunging headlong into the grimmest situation with the glee and recklessness of a child.

But for Hindle, each kilometer further east was one kilometer too far. She crumpled into her husband's arms, feeling grimy and uncivilized and she started to sob.

"What? What is this?" Lazar kissed her forehead and tried to push the loose strands of hair back from her eyes to no avail. "Are you sick of me already?" He tried to make her smile, while the driver peered over curiously at this strange, aristocratic woman, remembering those stories he had heard about, of all these rich, cultured Jews living west of Cracow, who resided in white, marble palaces illuminated through the night by electric candles, and slept with emeralds and diamonds under their pillows.

At that moment, Lazar caught sight of his home in the distance with its turning millstone and curing barns clearly visible beside the long, white main house.

"There! There. Hindella! It's our home. See? You will love it. I promise you, you will love it."

Lazar was up on his feet shouting and pointing when Hindle became aware of the smell, a scent mingling the sourness of milk with the acrid bite of vinegar that grew stronger in the air as the wagon approached Lazar's home. It did not disperse with the westerly breeze, but rather clung like rank nettles to the wind. Lazar did not seem to notice the odor, too excited by the sight of his family standing in the doorway to greet him.

"They're waiting for us. Everyone! Wait until they meet you Hindella. Wait until they meet my little countess!"

Secretly, Hindle had dreamt of this moment, an entrance of entrances, better than any theatrical scene she could recall, with the faces of Lazar's parents and his two aunts all looking on in admiration as she stepped from the carriage, marvelous and elegant in her West European manner and dress.

Instead, Isaac's mother arrived in Rovne in the summer of 1914 looking like a bedraggled refugee from a gypsy camp, deep in the swamps of Eastern Poland.

That night, Lazar's family began their examination of Hindle. Everyone had attempted to dress for this first dinner together, with Lazar in a starched collar, his mother in a high-waisted, billowing skirt, wrapped about with a flowery bow, and the two aunts, both widows, wearing stern black scarfs and blindingly white blouses.

"Oh, dear," she fussed, "did I forget to put out the right fork for the fish? Is this the way they do it in the city, Hindle?"

Poor Hindle, smiling, squirming, tried to laugh it off. "With such tender fish, we could eat it with a spoon, I'm sure."

And the aunts' eyes rolled up in dismay as they leaned toward each other, clucking and muttering over the last remark. And Rifka, the elder, snickered to herself, loudly.

"Who does she think she is? Too fancy for our stews and brown bread?"

Then, Lazar's father broke in to rescue Hindle from the clutches of the family, talking about all the new homes he was buying around the plant, all the new orders for boot leather and coat hides now that there were rumors of war, uttering over and over again how lucky Lazar was to be home at this time, with such a perfect wife.

"You see, Hindle, I called my boy back to help me with all this business and prosperity, but I really needed both of you, by my side, safe and secure along with the rest of my loved ones, just in case, just in case."

He would raise his voice to high dramatic pitch, and bang his silver-tipped cane on the floor for effect.

"No matter what ideas the Kaiser has about Rovne, I just know you would both be safer here, far from the craziness in Europe."

Then, with another slam of his cane: "So…here you both are, just like I planned. And when all the nonsense dies down, I promise both of you, that Lazar can return to his medical studies if he wishes, or remain here to grow rich and respected, just like me."

He kissed Hindle, embraced Lazar with a stocky, earthy hug, and half dragged his son away into their long, dark study while the ladies prepared for dessert.

All the time Lazar's father talked, he gripped his mahogany cane, a gift from some relative in America, like it was some sacred sceptre. But Lazar was more concerned about his wife, and his attention kept drifting to the gleam of the dining room where Hindle stood help—lessly in the center, facing the majestic forty-cup copper and silver Samovar that loomed menacingly on the sideboard. Hindle had seen Samovars in Zurich, but only as decorations in cafes and restaurants to lend an imperial Russian air to the place. Lazar's mother looked at Hindle, waiting for the new bride to carry out one of the basic chores of any Polish wife, to make tea for the evening. But, Hindle just stood gaping at the tall glistening urn, unable even to detect the small removable tea pot that nested in the top above the heating tube.

"Well, my dear. Do you think we can make some tea for the evening? My Lazar loved to drink gallons of it when he was a little boy. You wouldn't believe how much."

But Hindle didn't know where to begin with this copper-coiled, silver-clawed towering contraption. Aunt Faye, the youngest, giggled, while Aunt Rifka took Hindle's arm impatiently to guide her outside toward the water pump. Hindle resisted, not certain what connection a trip outdoors had with making tea. In her parents' comfortable apartment in Zurich, tea was simple matter of teapots and a warm stove. With Aunt Rivka practically pushing her outside, Hindle backed away, knocking into the dining table. For a moment, she caught Lazar's eyes in the other room. He was poised to rush from his chair and rescue her, but she quickly turned away, avoiding his glance, while she struggled against the desire to scream at these women and rush out to the road, to the west, back to the train, back to Zurich, where the air did not smell like a slaughterhouse and the dining rooms and cafes were full of cooks and waiters.

"Tell me, Hindle, dear," Aunt Rifka probed, "is it possible you don't know about tea? Lazar always needs his tea."

She gloated over Hindle's helplessness, knowing full well the demands of the Samovar exceeded the simple rituals of brewing tea: the pumping of the water into the wooden buckets, the filling of the giant urn; the shoveling of the hot embers from the fireplace into the copper "boot" that ran down the center of the Samovar; and then the tea pot itself, prepared and placed carefully on top of the Samovar like some regal crown. Aunt Rifka knew full well that encountering the Samovar for the first time was a trial by water and fire, which only true "natives" of this eastern world could master. Her own beloved late husband, Soloman, could pluck the hot embers from the hearth with his bare hands and place them in the Samovar for her. She was sure Hindle would never measure up to any one of the real family, not even when it came to making tea.

With his wife surrounded by the women, Lazar could hardly focus on his father's pronouncements. His father's cane cracked on the floor. His voice heightened dramatically, and then he would suddenly sit on the edge of the chair, shoulders back, spine stiff as a soldier, and announce a decision. That's how Lazar's life had been ruled in the past, by pronouncements! That's why he went to private school and spoke seven languages and, finally, was ordered by his father to take up medical study at the University of Zurich. His father determined the destiny of his son with the cane firmly in hand and spine straight as a birch, sitting suspenseful on the edge of the chair. With the certainty of a biblical patriarch, Lazar's father would scratch out his son's destiny on the clay floor with the tip of his cane as surely as prophets inscribed oracles on papyrus. But, this time, Lazar thought, his father had not included Hindle in his calculations, or the assassination of Archduke Ferdinand.

At first, however, even in Zurich, Lazar could hear the scraping of his father's cane all the way from Rovne and the shadow of its dictates across his path, controlling his every move. It was through his father's business contracts that Lazar was allowed to board with an Austrian-born merchant and his wife in a spacious Zurich apartment. The merchant had four daughters, the youngest being Hindle, and the whole family treated Lazar affectionately, like he was a long lost brother. The parents introduced him to the continental life of a Jew in western Europe, recognizing immediately Lazar's obvious intelligence and character. So, they set out to simply mold his manners and hone his sense of culture to a fine edge by introducing him to cafes and restaurants, theaters and concerts, and by shopping with him along the Bahnhofstrasse. With each sortie into the streets of Zurich, the parents would often bring along their oldest unmarried daughter, Ruth. She was the shorter, stockier, and thicker-featured than all the other daughters, but she was the oldest and carried with her an ample dowry and a fashionable trousseau that filled one streamer trunk and a cedar closet. Lazar's father had been aware through his original correspondence with the Zurich family of Ruth's desirability and availability. He confirmed his own interest in the match, but insisted that Lazar discover Ruth's desirability as a wife on his own.

Lazar was not told of any nuptial intentions, but her availability became increasingly obvious. With the hopes and investments of her parents settled on her, she began to accompany Lazar with greater frequency on his cultural and civilizing sojourns into the heart of Zurich, with the parents alongside, of course. And Ruth's parents would seemingly arrange each new social excursion to provide Lazar with at least one opportune moment to make a proposal, usually between tea and pastries, or the first and second act of some theatrical, or just before the maid brought the evening chocolate.

But, Lazar did not propose. When the parents deliberately left Ruth and Lazar alone at some cafe table to greet friends across the room, Lazar would start smiling silently and Ruth would grin back wordlessly. Then, the parents would return to recommend some flamboyant dessert like Bombe Glace with striped ice cream and raspberries in a tulip glass. While Lazar scooped up the ices, he would smile once again at Ruth over his spoon and she would grin back and blush over the raspberries.

Everyone assumed Lazar was inordinately shy with women. So, the parents would try again to arrange unprepared and relaxed settings for his inevitable proposal. At the theater, they would sit him next to Ruth so that he might laugh with her at the comedy or operette. During intermission they would leave them both in the corner of the lobby, but Lazar would only nod and mumble his approval of the first act and Ruth, biting the corner of her lip nervously, would nod back in agreement.

Finally, it became apparent to Ruth's father that Lazar was probably one of those "idiot savants" who excel exceedingly well in one are of study or talent, but remain incompetent in all ofter facets of life. Lazar was, after all, from the eastern part of Poland, where gypsies and bandits roamed.

The father concluded that Lazar would most likely become a doctor and settle once again in the wilds of his native country, ministering to farmers, gypsies and beggars. He was a lost cause as far as Ruth was concerned.

But, it was just about the time that the parents gave up on Lazar, that Hindle took up the cause. While Lazar would sit late into the night in the family's library, studying his anatomy text by the alcohol lamp, Hindle began joining him, knitting late into the night, on the other side of the desk. At first, they barely talked, and only pages turned and needles clicked late into the morning. But slowly, voices could be heard from behind the door. Hindle had found someone to take her seriously.

She began talking, at first about her silly schoolmates, and then her childhood, and soon she was bubbling away incessantly about her love of Yiddish musicals and Austrian operettas. Some nights, while Lazar rested between his study of the twelve cranial nerves and the circulatory system, Hindle would regale him with a simple Yiddish song, humming the melody quietly, and then whispering the words in a sweet, flutelike voice, just loud enough for Lazar to savor across the dim-lit desk: "In dem Bes Hamikdosh, in a vinkle heder, Zist di amono Bas Tsiyon alen."

Soon, the singing and the chatter carried throughout the house and Ruth protested that he little sister was disturbing Lazar's studies. The parents protested, but Lazar insisted he was happy to have the company in the late hours. It made his studies more bearable. And besides, her singing and gossiping kept him awake.

The nightly chatter and chirping became an occasional walk on weekends into the city itself, along the great lake. To Lazar, Zurich had always seemed a great, grey fort of a city, with tall, imposing walls and parapets of fog and ashy stone in a dim, perpetual drizzle. Its streets were like baffling mazes to keep intruders out and the discontented forever lost within its battlement. But Hindle's presence, her gentle chime of a voice, and her delicate smile, changed all that. Zurich seemed lush and tropical suddenly, green as the Polish woods and bright as Eden itself.

One day, they stopped to picnic by the Limnat River on a bank near the apple orchards and vineyards covering the shallow plateaus nearby. Hindle would hum as she handed Lazar some dark, sweet rolls, the color of charred potatoes, and cheese, then remember a funny story or a wish she had made when she was very young, and she would begin another delightful tale. But, this time, Lazar hushed her with his finger to her lips And he began to talk. He was tired of ventricles and cerebellums, bored with stratums of the skin and the flow of arterial rivers. Instead, he remembered and related elaborate stories of his own days in Poland with childhood friends, of fights with bullies in school who baited Jews in the market-place, and explorations of the treacherous marshes of Polessi. Soon, Lazar was exploding with tales and marvels of Rovne and the Sussenkess Woods, and his father's great house with giant millstones.

It went on like that for weeks. In the middle of this great medieval fortress of a city, resting in the shank of the Alps, at the center of modern Europe, this medical student from East-ern Poland could not stop talking about his little Polish town and the land about it. Up and down the Limnat River, around Lake Zurich, Lazar told Hindle story after story, adventure upon adventure, sharing secret wishes and dreams. Hindle became enraptured by Lazar's vision of his own country. She began to long for what he loved, for it seemed so free and sub-lime, and so irresistible in his telling. So irresistible that one day she took his hand and squeezed it lovingly as he talked. It was a signal Lazar could not ignore. The next day, in the apple orchard, by the river, he kissed her and asked her to marry him.

Ruth, at first, was quiet when Hindle told her, with Lazar by her side. But with Lazar at school, Ruth erupted angrily, ripping at Hindle's blouse, screaming at her face, sobbing and crying, and at one point, flinging Lazar's medical texts at the wall, then pouncing on the books to tear them apart. Hindle pulled her away and clutched the books protectively to her breast.

The war between the sisters went on for days. The parents hesitated to consent, sending urgent letters to Poland hoping that Lazar's father could write something that would force Lazar to his senses, accept protocol and marry the older daughter, as was expected. After all, Hindle was barely nineteen at the time and only a small paltry portion of the family estate had been settled upon her. She brought with her a meager dowry and barely a proper linen sheet or two in her trousseau, much less a vintage wedding dress. Compared to Ruth, Hindle came to marriage a beggar, in need of clothing and shelter.

But Lazar held firm, insisted, demanded and finally convinced the parents, impressed by his passion and confidence. The wedding was a quiet one, in the rabbi's chambers, with a small gathering that followed at Hindle's favorite cafe, where she could sing a song or two to her new husband. Ruth did not attend, but stayed at home, knitting in the library by the alcohol lamp.

A month after their August marriage, while still living in the apartment, Lazar and Hindle heard about the assassination of Archduke Ferdinand in some Adriatic city. But Lazar was too busy studying for his physiology exams and Hindle was more concerned about learning to cook the special flanken and dumpling stew her husband loved so much. They paid no attention to the course of political events or the rumors of war.

However, Lazar's father did follow the news and grew concerned. Finally, he sent a telegram asking his Lazar to return to Rovne with his wife. Letters followed, one after another. He claimed the threat of war and the presence of the Russian army on the border near Rovne increased the demand for leather parts and boot tops. He needed his son's help in running the tanning business and promised prosperity, property, and safety to both of them.

Lazar could hear the thud of his father's cane, the clear scratch of the tip of clay floor and knew his destiny was being altered, but he could not ignore the pronouncement. He knew what it meant and he weighed carefully the prestige and joy of medicine against the steady comfort and wealth of a leather manufacturer. It meant, most of all, a return to his beloved town, where he could show Hindle the locations of all his wondrous stories and let her touch the soil and feel the branches of the white birch trees against her face.

So, he left Zurich and medical school with Hindle and journeyed home, by train after train, and finally wagon, back to his birthplace, to family, to Rovne.

It struck him now, sitting in the dark of the study, watching his new wife stumble through the tasks of the Samovar, how far poor Hindle had traveled, not just in kilometers, but in everything. She was in an imaginary dining room, in an imaginary house, in an imaginary town. Nothing she had ever experienced before could have prepared her for this. It was all unreal and new. Lazar watched as she splashed water everywhere, trying to pour the basket into the Samovar, and cringed when she attempted to carry the copper shovel of hot embers to the great urn, spilling a hot coal on the way where it bounced toward Aunt Faye's skirt, practically setting it afire. Each moment, he felt an urge to grab Hindle and start back to Zurich. If only she turned to him and said with her eyes, "This cannot be. We must not stay a moment longer." But, she refused to admit her sense of helplessness; she would not run from tasks. Instead, she kept asking to the aunt's dismay, "Am I doing this right? You'll have to show me. This is all too new and different, but I'll get it right soon enough, I promise."

When Lazar's father pointed out with his cane the borders of his widening property and all the new houses newly acquired, Lazar had to go to the window and look out in the darkness with his father by his side.

"There will be a house for each child, I promise you. You will never have to worry about a home. Never. We'll have our own town someday."

It was then, that the tapered, sweet fingers of Hindle touched Lazar's shoulders. He turned. His wife stood there, her apron soaking wet, her face covered with soot and streaked with ash, her fingers singed and red. But she smiled proudly and announced to Lazar and her father-in-law, "The Samovar is hot. The tea is ready."

After this evening, Lazar thought, the Kaiser and Czar would be easy. His Hindle would prevail over all of them. She repeated, with authority, while the aunty and the mother glared at her in the flickering light of the dining room, "I made gallons of tea, just for you Lazar, so you can drink it all night."

She didn't even mind the smell of the skins any more. Hindle was truly home.

CHAPTER FOUR

MYSTERIES OF THE HEART

Isaac used the second floor library of his older brother's medical clinic on Skolynia Street as a refuge sometimes from snarling bullies who would chase him from school with rocks, shouting, "Juden Swine!" or "look at the insect!" Other times, Isaac would hide in the shadow by the small, stone-arched window of the library to catch a glimpse of some especially attractive and voluptuous female classmate. She would always be someone taller than Isaac, more brazen and forward, who loved to tease him and flirt with her eyes and lips. Shy and unsure, he could only watch such a girl secretly from his brother's window.

More often, Isaac would escape to the second floor study of the clinic just to sit among the impressive volumes of scientific texts and scholarly works his brother, Sol, had collected in his years as a research scientist in Cracow before he returned to become Rovne's most respected doctor. In that sunlit study just above the long hallway where Sol's patients sat on wooden benches waiting their turn, Isaac would pretend he was a famous doctor as well, and sit in the library's oversized leather chair with the great books spread out before him on his lap.

When Isaac was younger, the pages seemed covered with mysterious formulas and frighteningly long words made up of unpronounceable Greek, Roman, or High German syllables. But, lately, with Isaac already sixteen, the texts seemed less mysterious, the formulas increasingly familiar, and the words challenging puzzles to be solved. He could even pose an intelligent question to his brother about some word or some intricate formula.

But today, May 10, 1941, was different. Isaac wasn't rushing towards his brother's clinic because he was hiding from bullies, or planning to sneak forbidden glances at some flirtatious girl. He wasn't even interested in looking at a single medical text. On this unusually cold May afternoon, with a damp wind blowing across the Polessi Marshes, Isaac had come to his brother's clinic for another purpose.

As usual, he went to the side door, his face reddened by running in the cold, his fingers numb. Sol's wife, Lyuba, greeted him. Behind her, Isaac could see the familiar crowd of patients, sitting in the hall: Polish landowners in their fur-trimmed coats and beaver hats, Ukrainian farmers in thin linen blouses, Jewish merchants and shopkeepers in long cloth coats. Everyone came to his brother's clinic, from all walks and all stations of Polish life. But, today, Isaac wanted to see his brother before anyone else.

Lyuba saw the concern on the boy's face and the cold, impatient rubbing of his fingers. "Izzy, it's so cold out and you wear nothing. Shame on you."

"Why is Sol so busy today?" Isaac hung back at the door, jealously glaring at all the patients.

"Now, you know everyone comes to your brother. He is a great doctor."

"But Zayda needs him! Right away! Zayda can't come to the clinic so Sol has to go to the house. Right now! It's our Zayda who needs the great doctor more than anybody!"

Isaac's eyes welled up with tears and he continued to move about nervously, too embarrassed to let the patients see him in such a state. But Lyuba understood and drew him close to her in a comforting embrace, kissing the top of his head reassuringly.

"Now, now, you know your brother will never let anything hurt Zayda. He is doing everything that's possible. He loves his Zayda as much as you do. As soon as he closes the clinic, Sol will go back to the house and stay by his side. Like he has done every day since he took sick."

Isaac trembled for a second, all the emotion and anxiety surging up inside him, as he fought to keep from sobbing.

"I tell you what, Izzy. You go upstairs to the library and just wait. We'll all go back to the house together. Wouldn't that be best? Why go home alone now that you're here? Wait for us."

Lyuba understood exactly what Isaac was feeling and gave him an apple and a piece of goat cheese, and gently pushed him upstairs to the books. It was true. Isaac didn't want to go home alone. All day in school he thought about it and was afraid of walking into his house to find his grandfather even sicker than he had left him in the morning. Each day, it seemed, his grandfather had become thinner and weaker than the day before. Zayda's once solid and hefty face had grown increasingly smaller until it seemed to Isaac as if his grandfather was disappearing into the creases of the great feathery pillow beneath his head. It was like Isaac was watching some woodsman carve out a miniature of his grandfather's face and each day another splinter of the soft white pine fell away, another shaving of life and robustness was whittled off. He could not stand the grim look in his mother's eyes or the feeling of cold grief when he took his father's hand. Everyone was so tired and sad at home. And, besides, it had become unnaturally quiet, like his house had been deserted.

Once his Zayda's strong, booming voice would shake the walls, but now it was a hoarse whisper. And everyone else talked in the same low, hushed tones as grandfather. Nothing was familiar to Isaac any more. Grandpa's illness had changed it all.

Even his father worked longer hours and came home later and more exhausted. His mother would blame it on the Germans and Russians and all their "agreements." Two years before in the Fall of 1939, Poland had been carved up between the Russians and Germans, though Isaac didn't feel any different when it happened. The Russians took over the Volhynia region with all the woods and marshes and towns, just like that, and Rovne was suddenly Russian once again after twenty-five years of independence. With that, the Russians took over factories and schools and even the tanning plant. Now Lazar worked for the Russians. Isaac's mother, Hindle, would blame all their problems on "the Bolsheviks," hissing the word out loudly when no one else would dare say "Russians."

For Isaac, it was all a distant reality, gossip and an occasional radio broadcast on their kitchen console announcing new German victories and Russian triumphs. Slowly, the world of Rovne became as difficult to understand as his brother's medical textbooks. Isaac's own library, full of Burroughs, Scott, Stevenson and DeMauppasant still held a nostalgic charm for him. But, he felt the need to know more facts, more answers, and all the romances and adventures he had read belonged to another world receding faster and faster into the past.

A few nights after Zayda had been bedridden, the old man called Isaac to the bedside to chat. In the middle of a quiet conversation, his grandfather suddenly became agitated and then he started to laugh, pointing a finger at Isaac as he warned him, "Don't be fooled, Izzela. They say this is a phony war, that's all. They call it, what is it, a 'sitzkrieg'! Idiots! The Kaiser and the Czar could never agree on anything and they were family. They all want Poland for themselves. The Bolsheviks won't let us alone. You wait and see, my baby. Phony war! Ha!" His laughter turned into a fit of coughing and Isaac was quickly ushered out of the bedroom.

Even at school, this war that was no war had changed everything. Polish schoolmates were encouraged by the authorities to keep their eyes and ears open, to spy, to eavesdrop, and when anything heard sounded like an attack on Stalin or Hitler, they were to report it back to their teachers. If it was a minor insult, a slip of the tongue, the students would still get a reward of some hard candies. If they reported back serious attacks on their "leaders," bordering on "treason, sedition or betrayal," then the children would get Russian uniforms with shiny caps and a tin medal with Stalin's profile on it. Everything had begun to change.

One night, Isaac heard his Zayda shout as loudly as he could when someone tried to convince him he was going to outlive the entire family, "I know better! Everyone is crazy not to see! I'm glad I won't be around much longer. I couldn't stand living in the same country with those Nazi and Bolshevik goniffs! Spit on all of them!"

If his voice carried to the outside, Isaac feared some vicious schoolchild might report what his grandfather said, for a piece of hard candy or a shiny cap, and Zayda would be thrown in prison forever. It could not go on this way.

So, upstairs in his brother's library, Isaac began searching for a cure to his grandfather's sickness. If he could help make his grandfather healthy again, then the rest of the world might return to normal as well. Since Sol had told him it was his Zayda's heart, he looked up "heart" in all of the medical dictionaries and texts, drawing over and over as many diagrams of the heart as he could find. Soon, he was able to sketch in his sleep, ventricle and auricle, valve and chamber, arteries and veins. If it was his Zayda's heart, he could draw the problem and have Sol fix it. Once, his brother had let him listen through his stethoscope to the osculation of a patient's heart, a young Ukranian farmer, frightened by the instruments and white surgical jackets. Isaac nervously listened to what Sol had told him would be the "Lubb Dupp" "Lubb Dupp" sound, as the ventricle chambers contracted and the blood banged against the wall of the chest, and then ebbed, relaxing in a short, high-pitched tone. But, Isaac only heard a distant thump like a far-away train. If it was just Zayda's heart, Isaac thought, Sol has only to adjust a valve here, a tube there, and it would work right once again. After all, his grandfather needed only the smallest, bead-like pills to take if he felt bad. It couldn't be that serious.

Isaac continued the search on that cold May afternoon for some new word, some new diagram that might help. After all the years of studying his brother's books and listening to his brother tell patient after patient what to do with cuts and bruises, wounds and diseases, he refused to believe his Zayda's ailment had no simple solution. He looked over lists of symptoms and indications he had compiled with new names and new formulas, all dizzying and confusing. But Isaac kept searching, hoping tonight he could help Sol bring back the answer.

Then, he heard his brother call him. It had always been easy for Isaac to listen to voices downstairs, his brother's voice carried even from the examination room. But this time,

Sol sounded more insistent, disturbingly impatient. He had rushed through his patients and was anxious to get back to grandfather. Isaac was bothered by the sound of urgency in his brother's voice, so he rushed downstairs into the hall, outside the office where Sol was waiting with his long, dark coat already on. Lyuba was by his side, ready to leave as well.

When Sol saw Isaac, he smiled, almost sadly, and took his brother's hand. "Tell me, Professor, have you figured out all the diseases yet or will you leave me a few to cure? What's that?" Sol caught sight of notepaper Isaac clutched in his hands. It was one of Isaac's drawings. Sol took it gently from his brother's grasp and studied it seriously. "An artist too, I see."

"It's Zayda's heart," Isaac shyly admitted.

Sol looked at his wife, suddenly touched by Isaac's profound efforts, his eyes misting, his face softening into a look of poignancy and sadness. He turned to Isaac, "Don't worry. It's a fine heart you have drawn. Zayda is in good shape if that's the picture of his heart. Come on now, Izzy, enough scholarship and research for today, don't you think? Let's take you home."

At the house, the candles seemed unusually dim. Hindle held Isaac at her side in the kitchen, humming some sad melody, while preparing the pot of tea for the samovar. His father had not yet returned from the plant even though it was dark and a fine mist had begun to fall. The rest of the household filed in and out of the bedroom where his grandfather rested. Isaac, seated in the dining rom, watched, with the strange feeling that his beautiful house was fading, losing its color, as if the walls and furniture and even the samovar were growing gray and transparent. While Hindle and Sol, Lyuba and Aunt Rifka, walked in and out of the bedroom whispering, Isaac could see the colors draining. Even at night, his house with its ornately framed paintings and gilded mirrors, its breakfront full of crystal and gold-lipped glasses, always seemed so bright and luminous. But, tonight it grew duller and duller, until there was nothing but shadows.

When Lazar finally arrived in his wagon, he didn't wait for his son to run and greet him. He came right inside, still stained and soaked from his day's work and quickly washed up without saying a word to anyone.

Then, the procession into grandfather's bedroom became even more tense and regular. In they went, family member after family member, then out again, sobbing or quietly sobbing. What Isaac did not know was that his Zayda, near death, was announcing to each loved one his or her inheritance, whether a plot of land, a house, monies or possessions. Even at his end, Isaac's grandfather was controlling destinies with love and pride, without the strength to lift his cane.

Then, it was Isaac's turn. His mother took him by the hand and led him into the large bedroom. It has been his parents' bedroom until grandfather had become sick. There, propped up on many pillows, was his beloved Zayda, smaller, whiter and more frail than ever. Isaac noticed the dark, brass-tipped can resting by the zinc-topped bedstand. His grandfather nodded and Isaac was gently urged by his mother to approach. Isaac stood by the bed, stiffly, his heart pounding.

"Child, I can barely whisper. Closer."

Isaac leaned forward, putting one knee on the bed while his Zayda took his hand, encircling it with thin, feeble fingers that at one time could grip Isaac so tightly it would hurt. Even his grandfather's hand had become smaller, dainty and slight like an infant's.

"You have been studying hard to make me better."

His grandfather looked down at him from a ledge of pillows supporting his back. "Sol told me. Thank you, Izzela. You are a fine boy. Someday, you will cure everyone. Now listen, I leave…that special house. The one we rent to those no-goodnicks from the theater. It's your mother's favorite house. Keep it for her. Now, one more thing. Closer."

He tried to lift his head off the pillow to get closer, but he had no strength. "My cane. You have that too. It is from America. You will not stumble if you use it."

Then, his grandfather sank back into the creases of the pillow, sighing, his eyes fluttering and he started to clear his throat loudly. Hindle and Aunt Rifka ran up to the bed and Lazar led Isaac out of the bedroom quickly. That was the last moment Isaac spent with his Zayda. He died before morning.

At the Gochov Synagogue, the crowds for Isaac's Zayda were impressive. Over five hundred pressed into the great synagogue and another hundred milled outside. Chief Rabbi Mahofit mounted the raised circular dais at the center of the temple to deliver a forty minute eulogy, and when the plain wooden coffin arrived by wagon at the cemetery, the rabbi delivered another speech outside lasting fifteen minutes, with over a thousand friends and citizens lining the road to the gravesite and surrounding the cemetery.

A week of mourning followed, with everyone sitting on old boxes in a darkened and draped house, the mirrors shrouded and furniture covered in sheets. Isaac had never been so close to the rituals of death before, but with the week of mourning, the reality and finality of his grandfather's passing settled in. He began to consider the death of all his loved ones and the thought made him panic inside. He wanted to stop it all just as it was and keep everyone exactly as they were.

Each day, friends and townspeople would file through the house, carrying food and flowers to pay their respects. The Polish fireman renting the house down the road brought special sesame candies and Turkish nougats, the Catholic priest from St. Ignatius entered with a bow, and presented a wheel of cheese. Even the dogcatcher, Godtz, showed up with his stocky, square-jawed wife, his giant of an assistant named "Chlop" with beefy arms, droopy eyes and a wild mane of blond hair that fell to his shoulders, and his big-breasted, stringy-haired daughter. Isaac's buddies showed up as well, with Hagar peering constantly at all the food through his bushy eyebrows and Morris gallantly striding about trying to express his condolences with a stammer.

Godtz' daughter, a year older than Isaac, began to smile alluringly when she saw the spaciousness of the house and realized the dimensions of Isaac's family holdings. She wore a cheap, green blouse that had a silky sheen to it in spots where it had been scrubbed too hard, and she pressed close to Isaac no matter where he turned, her bosoms soft on his back as she leaned toward him again and again. Isaac had seen her before in town and once near school, and even dreamt of her in a strange way that he could not understand. In the dream, she was nursing two babies at once near the broken fountain by the marketplace and the townspeople lined up to give her more babies to nurse; there were children everywhere, held up in the air, waiting to suckle on her breasts. He remembered the dream all too vividly now, and her sudden intimacy with him in his own house made him burn with shame and frustration.

Each time he moved away, she found him, pressing once again on his back, her lips large and red, her skirt and blouse brushing against his arm and leg. Finally, facing her, he tried to talk but his words stumbled out and she giggled. Just at that moment, Morris approached, and seeing his friend's panic, tried to rescue him.

"Is...Is...Isaac, Co...cou...could you come...come to the kitchen, p...p...please..."

At the sight of Morris struggling with his words, Godtz' daughter burst out in shrieks of cruel, savage laughter, humiliating Morris. Her brutal laughter infuriated Isaac and the look of her face, contorting into an ugly and coarse mask of derision, repelled him. Pushing her away roughly, he put his arm around Morris and walked away, certain he would never dream of the dogcatcher's daughter again.

Even after the week of mourning was over and the shrouding sheets removed from the mirrors and furniture, the house still felt different, the color drained from the walls, the sunlight only a pale, gray shadow falling across the floor.

Then one night, just before bedtime, Isaac's mother came into his room carrying grandfather's cane. It had been forgotten in all the ceremonies and rituals and overlooked in the distribution of grandfather's estate. Her sudden appearance reminded Isaac of times before when his mother would come to his bedside at night and sing a song. But all that had changed lately.

This night, Hindle came into her son's room smiling once again, offering the cane to him. "It is yours now."

"But, Mama, I don't need it."

"Even if it stays in the corner, it will help." She placed the cane at the foot of his bed, leaning it against the wall. As she turned to leave, Isaac had to announce the secret of his last visit with Zayda.

"Mama, Zayda gave me that house where all the actors live."

"I know, baby. When you're older, not now."

"Mama, I promise whenever you want that house, I'll kick out all the singers. You have a better voice than all of them put together anyway."

Hindle smiled, touched and flattered. Then she sat down at the edge of the bed, holding Isaac's hand and kissing each finger like she did when he was very young.

"Now, sha, sha, it's very late."

Then, quite naturally, she started to sing softly to her son. It was Isaac's favorite song, the one about the rabbi dancing joyously and the children watching without a sound.

"Sha, shtil, mach nish kein gevalt..." she sang with her finger to her lips dramatically, hushing Isaac and the whole world so that the rabbi could dance in peace. "Sha, shil..."

When she left the room, Isaac kept humming the melody to himself, content and serene, knowing that the house would soon be bright and luminous again. Just before he went to sleep, he took the cane from the foot of his bed and placed it at the head, next to his bedstand, just as Zayda would, and he fell asleep with one hand touching it.

CHAPTER FIVE

WHITE BIRCHES

In the weeks following the death of his grandfather, Isaac sensed a reluctance on the part of his parents to rush back into everyday chores and labors. Then with the coming of June, the summer weather settled in, and the days grew hot and still, driving everyone outside late into the night to sit and talk. Even with the reek of the curing skins hanging heavy in the air, the family sat outside in the twilight, enjoying cup after cup of tea, with Isaac on the ground by his father's chair, listening.

Some nights they'd play the radio console so loud, even the neighbors would come by to hear the latest news or listen to music from Vilna or Grodno. But on most nights, Hindle and Lazar would just talk and reminisce. In the face of disturbing rumors about Nazi activity in German-occupied towns, along with the political gossip Lazar picked up on his business trips to neighboring towns, it was comforting for Isaac's parents to retreat back into the certainty of the past. After all, Lazar would roar with laughter, once you survive one "war to end all wars," what's one more war or less. Isaac was impressed by how indomitable and resolute his parents seemed in all their stories. Even more surprising to Isaac, listening in the twilight with only the clicking of crickets and the turning of the millstones as background, the ordeals and hardships were spoken of as cherished and endearing memories, adding to his image of his parents' resiliency and endurance.

One night, Lazar recalled his whole experience in World

War I, fighting Austria and Germany as a forced recruit in the Russian army. Even though Hindle was from Austrian descent and Lazar had no personal devotion to the Russian Czar, he still thought of it as his war with the "Huns." Pressed into service early in 1915, right after Hindle had given birth to Sol, Lazar marched and marched for weeks before seeing action. Then on a battlefield near Presburg in Austria, he had his first and last battle.

Most of the time, Lazar remembered, was spent knee deep in mud hiding behind trenches and breastworks made of sandbags and timber, when, finally, an officer blew a whistle and his division was ordered to attack. Listening to his father tell the story, Isaac assumed this was the major battle of the war. Lazar added extra artillery shells, bursts of cannon fire, flashes of incendiaries and waves of sulfurous smoke to accompany his description. As Lazar pictured it, all of Europe seemed to hang in the balance as he charged across the battlefield toward the enemy trenches. Storming the barbed wire barricades of the Austrians, Lazar lead into a trench of the "Huns," taking one poor Austrian completely by surprise. The young Austrian had been stunned by the concussion of a nearby explosive and been left behind in his battalion's retreat. He was dazed and confused when Lazar came upon him. Lazar quickly raised his rifle, took aim at the young man's heart and was about to press the trigger when the Austrian, realizing his fate, dropped to his knees, bowed his head, prepared to receive the bullet, and began to chant the Hebrew words, "Shema Yishrael, Adonoi…" Over and over again he recited the holiest prayer of the Jewish faith with Lazar standing above him, rifle now pointing at the back of his head. "Hear me, O Israel, the Lord our God, the Lord is One…"

In the midst of the smoky haze and throbbing glow of distant fires, Lazar stood transfixed by the pious sound of a kinsman, a fellow Jew. He could not squeeze the trigger. Instead, he stood there while the Austrian continued to chant, then bewildered by his own emotions, Lazar backed away, indifferent to direction or imminent danger, until he walked inadvertently into the enemy camp and was captured without a shot. He spent the next year as a prisoner in Presburg, working as a military baker and living in a private boarding house taken over by the army, his war with the Huns over in one prayer.

Hindle, leaning over at the end of Lazar's war story to kiss him, added the final chapter, recounting the day Lazar returned. It was even hotter and more oppressive than this summer weather on that day when Lazar suddenly appeared at the doorstep, returning from captivity. Hindle started to scream and dance, then sing with joy. Quickly, Lazar greeted everyone, then escaped with Hindle into the depths of the Sussenkess, where they lost themselves for the entire day in the shadowy coolness of the white birch. It was as romantic and memorable as their days on the Limnat River in Zurich when Lazar courted Hindle for the first time. On that summer day in the Susenkess, Hindle and Lazar acted like passionate young lovers once again in the hallow of the forest.

It was difficult for Isaac to imagine his father and mother romantically inclined even in the house, much less in the middle of the woods, but he was touched by the affectionate memory and marveled at their shared joy. However, he did know, first hand, how much his father adored the Susenkess since is had become tradition for Lazar to take his son on a summer picnic in the forest for the past few years.

They were precious journeys for Isaac, moments of solitude with his father that allowed Lazar to share all he had learned about nature and survival, courage and will. On one trip, Lazar pointed out the right mushrooms to eat, "only the purest white, not the mottled, not the sullied or the gray." On another, he taught Isaac how to boil poison ivy carefully to prepare a soup of amazing vitality, supplying most of the iron needed for vigor. Some of his knowledge came from war time, some from business trips where he encountered gypsies and recluses, eccentric hermits and hunters, all sharing their observations with Lazar, who passed them on to his son.

At the end of the long evening of storytelling, Lazar resolved that he and his son should picnic once again in the Susenkess. Isaac rejoiced and dreamed for the next few nights of exploring lush, vine covered jungles with his father.

Finally, the day came, and the wagon was loaded with food and cider and special mandel bread baked by Isaac's aunt. As they bumped and rattled in the old wagon, waving good-bye to Hindle and Aunt Rifka, Isaac realized this was the first picnic trip without his grandfather waving goodbye to them with his cane in the air as they drove past the millstones. But, everything else was the same: the howls of laughter and shrieks as Lazar rushed the wagon down small hills and over rougher and rougher terrain; the songs they both tried to sing, always off-key, ending in laughter; finally, all the wondrous stories that Lazar told about his favorite biblical characters, stories he changed and embellished until Moses and Jonah became Polish and Canaan and the Red Sea became Rovne and the Bug River.

With each story, whether it was about Jonah or Moses or even Abraham, Lazar always had the same point to make, "When you know that the Lord is calling you in your heart, Izzela, always volunteer. Moishe volunteered and he made it all the way to the promised land, which, by the way, looks a little like the Susenkess in summer. When God calls, always say "yes," otherwise you end up like Jonah, in the belly of a giant sturgeon in the Bug River."

Isaac loved the liberties his father took with such stories and often incidents were added that came from Lazar's own adventures on the road.

This day, bouncing up and down on the rickety wagon, Lazar tried to draw a parallel between Abraham's willingness to sacrifice his beloved Isaac, and Zayda's consent to let Lazar fight in the Russian army. "It all worked out, didn't it? Because Zayda said 'yes' to the Czar." Isaac had great difficulty with the analogy, but he never questioned any point his father made.

Nearing the woods, Lazar stopped to pay a call on Godtz, the dogcatcher, to remind him of his overdue delivery of skins. Lazar often loaned money for goods not yet delivered and Godtz had already run up a substantial debt. They stopped at the high fence surrounding Godtz' yard, a fence made of barbed wire and pointed stakes. Refuse littered the grounds, inside and outside, and always, there were howls and yelping and long moans from the stray dogs within. It was a hideous and ugly place for anyone to live, even stray animals. Godtz came to the door, dressed in splattered and torn overalls, wearing a mud-caked ski cap. He looked at Lazar, almost sweetly, then down at Isaac with a stern glance, but Isaac's father went about his business quickly and simply, able to cope with any situation. Isaac could not ignore the meanness of the man and his surroundings. Out of the corner of his eye, Isaac saw Chlop's tall, hulking figure stalking about in the open yard. He was dragging a shaking, frightened mastiff by a short rope and holding a hefty tree limb in the other hand. Isaac shuddered and looked away, toward the inside of the house. In the darkness, he saw the daughter, clutching a thin blanket loosely around her body. She smiled and let a portion of the blanket fall away, exposing her shoulder. He turned back to his father quickly, avoiding her eyes, as Lazar attempted to fix a date for delivery of Godtz' promised skins. Even with his sweet, sick smile, Godtz' seemed unusually arrogant and stubborn that day, uncrushed, unconcerned. Finally, he agreed that by next week, he would deliver the skins. At that instant, Chlop appeared, standing behind Isaac and his father. He still held the tree limb at his side and Isaac thought he saw blood stains on the ugly coat of dog hides that Chlop wore over his giant frame. But Lazar showed not a flutter of concern, and jotted down calmly in his account book the date agreed on for delivery, while Isaac winced and cowered in the shadows of Chlop's menacing figure.

When they finally departed, Lazar took Isaac's hand and squeezed it. "No more business, I promise." Feeling the sweat and heat of fear in Isaac's palm, Lazar smiled, reassuring his son, "You're right to be afraid, Izzela. Godtz would kill anything for a bit of gold, but I'm the only one in the whole country willing to buy his nasty skins, so business is business even with barbarians."

He kissed Isaac on the side of the cheek, then rubbed his son's head playfully as they continued toward the Susenkess.

In a few minutes, it came into view, the deep, thick forest of white birch. It began at the top of a small rise and stretched back across the horizon as far as the eye could see, shimmering and brilliant in the hot afternoon sun. The unbroken life of birches, set densely together across the slopes, and the white sanctity of the bark, always reminded Isaac of some sacred temple wall, guarding and preserving the promise of paradise within.

NOTES ON THE CREATION OF:

THE RESETTLEMENT OF ISAAC
AND THE FIVE CHAPTERS

THE PLAY

Though I began my play, "The Resettlement Of Isaac," as a theatrical adaptation of my novel, "Isaac," my creative instincts soon centered on an elderly Isaac consumed by the haunting, romantic memory of his first love with a Russian Christian nurse in the Partisan Brigade he had joined a year after he miraculously survived the 1941 Nazi massacre of his family, friends and over twenty-thousand Jews from Rovno, Poland.

I changed the nurse's original name, Ducia, to Anya to create a new contemporary counterpart, Anna, a young German-American Christian, who had become Isaac's protective and compassionate neighbor in Manhattan many decades after the war.

In the play, I imagined that Anna's emotional immersion in Isaac's handwritten accounts of his courage and romance in the Polish woods instilled a deep affection for her aging Jewish neighbor.

In some way, my invention of Anna's intimate identification with Isaac's handwritten pages was similar, in reality to mine when the real Isaac during our first meeting, entrusted such pages to me. Thus began my own imagined journey through Isaac's life, which led to the writing of my novel, "Isaac." Therein lie the seeds of creation and imagination.

Since the memory of the elderly Isaac in the play shuttles back and forth between his past love, Anya, and his present relationship with the German-American, Anna, the similarity of the names merge dramatically in his mind.

Once rehearsals began for the elaborate stage reading of the play, the performance by the young, brilliant actress, Annemarie Hagenaars, playing both Anya and Anna, convinced my director, Robert Kalfin, of the theatrical power inherent in my creative choice of names.

I also took liberties with other names from my novel, "Isaac." I conflated some of the characters, changed some events, all in the name of theatrical economy and dramatic exigences.

But most importantly, I had to flash forward to imagine an elderly Isaac at the end of his days. It was a creative necessity, since the Isaac I remember through our many meetings in his Bronx apartment in the late 1980's was of an energetic man in his 70's, still vital and alert.

Then, many months after our last meeting, Isaac sent me a postcard announcing that he had moved from his co-op city apartment in the Bronx to Florida and would reside there for the rest of his life. Unfortunately, both personal and professional conflicts kept me from seeing him again.

So, after his death and later, after the publication of "Isaac," inspired by his wartime experiences, I realized the creative demands of my new play, "The Resettlement of Isaac," meant I had to create and imagine an aging Isaac out of whole cloth.

Nevertheless, from the creative threads of my imagination, I hope I remained true to the innate qualities of the Isaac I knew, a man I so admired and so vividly remembered from our many meetings.

THE CHAPTERS

The five prose chapters included with the play depict the life of a young Isaac before the outbreak of World War II. I had deliberately left out these chronologically earlier chapters from the original "Isaac," thinking my account in the book should begin with the Nazi invasion of Poland.

But these chapters seem to me now, more than ever, essential to understanding the mindset and the character of young Isaac, his family and friends before the advent of war. They provide a glimpse of the relatively peaceful, sometimes idyllic culture of Isaac's youth leading up to the eve of war and the eventual Nazi massacre of all that Isaac held sacred. They create a significant tone and mood of family life just before the horrors of war tear all asunder.

I was fortunate that my editor and publisher, Lauren Grosskopf, agreed as well that these chapters form a fitting and necessary prelude to both my novel, "Isaac," and my play, "The Resettlement of Isaac."

AN INTERVIEW WITH LONDON'S JEWISH TELEGRAPH, JANUARY 2018 expands on 'Notes,' as well as includes the experience of meetings with Isaac Gochman and the challenges in writing Isaac.

THIRTY years ago, New York playwright Robert Karmon first met Holocaust survivor Isaac Gochman, who wanted his amazing story to be told.

Last week, Robert finally published his first novel, *Isaac,* based on Gochman's life.

The 78-year-old explained the decades-long delay.

He said: "In the late 1980s, my agent put me in touch with Isaac. I didn't believe Isaac's story at first. He was in his 70s. I went to his home in the Bronx. As I sat down in his little kitchen, he started talking about his experiences surviving the massacre in Rovno, Poland."

In 1941, more than 20,000 Jews from the city were shot and buried in trenches. Among the victims were Isaac's parents and aunt.

Wounded Isaac, who was then only 16, was buried alive, only to later miraculously emerge, naked. After surviving months of wandering alone around forests, Isaac joined a band of Polish partisans.

The group included a nurse Ducia, with whom Isaac fell in love. Sadly she became ill giving birth to Isaac's child and was never seen again after she was taken away for hospital treatment.

Broken-hearted Isaac was proclaimed a hero by the invading American army after saving them from a Nazi insurgency.

Robert, professor emeritus of literature and creative writing at Nassau Community College in Garden City, Long Island, told me: "The story sounded so incredible at first that I didn't believe it. But Isaac started sharing photos and hand-written notes with me and it became obvious that it had really happened to him.

"Yet he was such a sweet, incredibly tranquil individual. I kept coming back to him once every two weeks. We began to put together some notes to turn the story into a novel. I was at his place at least 10 times over the next few months. Eventually I began writing the book. I shared the first few chapters with him. Then he moved to Florida. My agent died and we lost touch. But he had left me all his material."

The writing of Isaac went on Robert's backburner as he concentrated on writing plays and teaching creative writing. Nevertheless, over the years Robert kept returning to it.

He said: "As I was nearing the end of the novel, I tried to trace Isaac. I had lost his address. I found a different Isaac Gochman. But eventually I discovered that he had died in 1993. I was disappointed. I would have loved to have shared the book with him. I think he would have been happy. He had seen the first few chapters. Those were the most difficult ones."

The first chapters of the book describe the horrific Rovno massacre. The task of writing them was made difficult for Robert, not only because of horrific nature of the material, but because Robert's fear of flying made it impossible for him to actually visit Poland.

Robert, who is married with two daughters and three grandchildren, said: "I have never visited places which are monuments to the horrors of the Holocaust. But I did a lot of research. As a writer I projected myself into that world. It was difficult writing the first few chapters about the death march and Isaac's survival from the grave in the trench from which he climbs out naked. It was the most difficult writing I have ever done.

"It was a privilege to deal with it, but there was also a feeling that somehow it was beyond me. It took me a long time to get it right without exploiting it and becoming too graphic, but at the same time being as true as possible."

Robert added: "It was another element of the Holocaust. The death camps have become almost tourist attractions as monuments so people will never forget. But it is very hard to signify by monuments, people like Isaac's parents, who were buried in trenches in horrifying massacres. The Nazis threw quick lime over them and they were forgotten forever."

Robert, who has worked on screenplays for Columbia Pictures, CBS and Eddie Murphy Productions, continued:

"The things Isaac told me helped me understand it. Then I had to go back and search for texts about the forest. Somehow I created a real world I had not visited. The book becomes a kind of testimony or legacy for Isaac.

"Whatever I wrote, I heard Isaac always whispering in my ear. He was such an impressive and wonderful man.

He gave me permission to make it fictional and add my own insights and literary style. I could not have done it without him. I wish I could have seen him again so I could have shared the novel with him."

Isaac was given honorary citizenship of America for having saved the lives of American soldiers. He was granted a prestigious job in the US Postal System, where his knowledge of five languages came in handy.

By the age of 16, not only had Isaac become a linguist, but he also had medical knowledge from helping out his older brother Dr Sol Gochman, a popular Rovno doctor, who was shot for not carrying out the Nazis' instructions.

Even though he married and had a family in America, Isaac never forgot his first love, Ducia.

Robert has also adapted Isaac's story into the play *The Resettlement of Isaac. Isaac* is published by Pleasure Boat Studio.

ROBERT KARMON

IS AN AWARD WINNING PLAYWRIGHT, PUBLISHED POET, SHORT STORY WRITER AND PUBLISHED SCREENWRITER, who has worked on screenplays for Columbia pictures, CBS and Eddie Murphy Production. He was a member of Playwrights Horizon and Edward Albee's Playwrights Unit. His plays have been staged at Brown University, New York's Playwrights Horizons, where both his plays, "Demons" and "The Conditioning of Charlie One," were performed. His play, "The Waiting Room…" about the tragic life of 20th Century physicist, Paul Ehrenfest, was chosen by Urban Stages theatre for their "New Works for a New Season" and was later staged at The Workshop Theatre Company as part of their "Plays in Progress" program. His play "Caliban and Miranda," won Atlanta's Clayton State Theatre International Playwriting award. He has seen his plays staged at La Mama's Extension Theatre, and Long Island's Arena Players and in many regional theatres around the country. As a Professor of Literature and Creative Writing, he has taught at Temple University, Queens College, Hunter college, and is currently Professor Emeritus of Literature and Creative Writing at Nassau Community College in Garden City, Long Island. His book, *Isaac* was published by Pleasure Boat Studio in 2017. He is married with two daughters and three grandchildren.